About the Author

Kenneth (Ken) Ansell is an agriculturalist and farmer turned professional artist, who graduated from Durham University and completed his two years of National Service as a second lieutenant in a transport company before starting his working career in Agricultural Education in Cornwall, and, eventually, Devon. A keen horseman, he has experience in breeding and schooling young horses together with point-to-point racing and hunting. He has a small farm on the edge of Dartmoor where he lives with his wife and family. Now in his eighties, Ken rides regularly and still does his share in the stable yard.

To see more of Kenneth's books and his paintings,
visit www.kennethansell.co.uk

Also by Kenneth Ansell

Pendogget's Mare (*Filament Publishing*, 2015)
The Horse Traders (*Filament Publishing*, 2017)

The Fox

Kenneth Ansell

Published by
Filament Publishing Ltd
16, Croydon Road, Beddington,Croydon,
Surrey, CR0 4PA, United Kingdom
+44 (0)20 8688 2598
www.filamentpublishing.com

First edition published 1979.

This second edition published 2018.

ISBN 978-1-912635-45-0

Printed by IngramSpark.

All characters are fictitious.
Any resemblance to anyone, living or dead, is coincidental.

CHAPTER 1

CLEGG GRANGER scanned Ravenscoombe from the granite boulders that edged Dartmoor to the misty outline of Colspit Wood where the farm boundary ended, but there was no sign of his flock. He sought the shelter of some rocks and pushed back his sou'wester to let the rain wash through the dark stubble of his newly grown beard. It had been a hard climb and he leant against his long crook, watching the grey gusts billow and swirl between the steep sides of the coombe.

A black and white collie appeared out of the dead bracken and flopped, panting, beside him. "Well, they're not here, Skipper," Clegg said quietly. "God, will it never stop raining?"

He knew his little flock were close to lambing and he wanted to bring them down into the sheltered meadows by the farm before the weather worsened. Now he feared they had strayed out of the coombe on to the open moor where gathering would be much more difficult. "Just my luck," he muttered to himself.

He moved out of the shelter with the collie at his heels and turned to face the storm once more. Suddenly, a grey speck far down in the coombe caught his attention. It was a sheep for certain, and he hoped that where he found one he would find the others.

The way down was steep through knee-high bracken not yet flattened by the winter snows, for the weather had been kind until Christmas. Several times he slipped on hidden rocks so that by the time he reached the bottom, he was already saturated from the waist down.

The ewe was alone, which to Clegg meant only one thing: she was about to lamb or had already done so. One glance told him that the latter was the case and he began to look for the lamb, calling Skipper to heel in the hope that the ewe might lead them to it, if a fox hadn't got there first. The ewe ran to the edge of the stream which tumbled from the high ground in a series of miniature waterfalls. Now it was swollen with flood water, and where cattle had broken the banks to make a drinking place, Clegg saw the lamb. It lay among the stones and black mud like a screwed-up piece of dirty white rag, its hind legs drifting to and from in the back eddies. Even as he watched, it was caught up by the current and swept into the turmoil of brown water at the head of the next waterfall. In an instant, Clegg was in the water up to his knees, his crook ready to catch the lamb as it passed, then with a quick sideways lunge, he snatched the limp body and thrust it inside his coat.

Scrambling up the bank on all fours, he sat down to get his breath before taking out the lamb and holding it to his chest to feel for the faint tinge of warmth that would denote that life was still there. Slowly, his lips parted and for a brief moment his wind-chapped face relaxed. He got up and took the lamb over to the ewe to let her smell it, then, unbuttoning his oilskins, jacket and shirt, he put the cold, wet body next to his skin and, after emptying the water from his wellington boots, set off in the direction of the farm.

He reached a track and paused to make sure the ewe was following. The way now lay between drystone walls which took the sting out of the wind and helped Skipper, who was bringing up the rear, to keep the ewe close to Clegg. Inside his shirt, the morsel of life began to feel warm, and although there was still no movement, he felt certain it was not a dead thing he carried. He quickened his pace, the wind billowing his oilskins as he limped with bruised shins between the black streaming ruts.

Ravenscoombe Farm was set into a fold of the coombe, sheltered from the prevailing westerly winds and fronted by the only flat ground on the farm. Behind the house, small fields rose steeply to the road above, those nearest the house showing green where the land had been improved and more productive grasses sown, while those higher up were brown with tussocks and bracken. Whenever Clegg walked up the track, he saw those fields, reminding him how much work there was yet to do.

The gale was suddenly lost as he pushed through the gate that led into the yard. He propped it open while Skipper chivvied the sheep through, then banged it shut and crossed the yard to a range of stone loose boxes which made up one side of a square - the shippon, cattle yards and house comprising the other sides. Opening a door, he drove the ewe in, and after making sure the bolt was secure, he hurried to the back door of the house with Skipper at his heels.

The kitchen felt warm after the cold outside. Unbuttoning his oilskins, Clegg walked over to the old-fashioned kitchen range and poked the embers before making up the fire. He opened the oven door and placed the lamb just inside on a meat dish, leaving the door propped open with the poker. Next, he fetched a bottle of gin from the dresser and, taking a teaspoon from the unwashed breakfast things, he filled it and poured the contents into the lamb's mouth. Finally, telling the dog to stay, he went outside again to give a handful of corn to the distressed ewe, feeling her udder to ensure that it was healthy and full of milk. He returned to the warmth of the kitchen, took off his oilskins and wellingtons and slumped wearily into a chair.

Skipper came over to put his nose on his master's knee, and Clegg fondled his ears. "Well, that's the first of the lamb crop," he said. "Let's hope we have good luck with them this year."

Clegg knew he was taking a risk lambing earlier than was normal in the locality, but it was a risk he had to take if he was to make the farm pay. He stretched his long legs towards the fire and watched his trousers steam. He was used to being wet. His early years at sea had made sure of that. He thought of how Cathy would have made him change immediately, and the memory brought a frown. Well, Cathy wasn't here anymore. She had walked out on him and that was that. He pushed the dog away and stood up stiffly, then he turned and went upstairs, leaving a trail of wet footmarks across the stone flags.

The midday meal of cold meat, bread and pickles was washed down with two large mugs of hot sweet cocoa. Clegg turned on the radio, checked his watch and waited for the weather forecast. The announcer's unperturbed voice spoke the familiar words: "Portland, Plymouth, north-westerly gale force eight, moderating four or five ... snow showers in coastal areas ... "

He switched off and sat listening to the rising wind. The old formula for a bad blow, he thought, and went over to the barometer which hung on the wall by the back door. For a moment he studied it, then tapped the glass and grunted. It had been falling steadily for two days and he thought of the old sailors' rhyme: "Fall slow, long blow." He grimaced and prepared to go out again.

He was about to lift the latch when a rattle from the oven made him turn in time to see the lamb topple out of the meat dish as it scrambled to stand up. He went over and retrieved it. "Nearly forgot you, little feller," he said. "Another ten minutes and you would have been a hot supper. Time you went back to your mum."

The ewe made soft throaty noises as Clegg put the lamb against her flank. He waited until instinct and her gentle nudges prompted it to seek the distended udder, and not until the wriggling tail indicated that the teat had been found did he leave them.

A loose slate rattled on the roof of the loft above the shippon and Clegg made a mental note to fix it. He decided too that he must do something about the yard which was uneven and pockmarked where running water had gouged out loose particles. One day, he thought, the yard would be concreted and brushed clean, with blue paint on the loose box doors and a white gate ... His reverie was broken by Skipper's cold nose nudging his hand. "Come on then, let's get going," he said.

Dark cloud banks over the moor softened and spread until the whole sky was an even grey tinted with yellow. The wind eased as man and dog laboured towards the head of the coombe where moor and sky became one. Both sensed the drop in temperature, but only the dog could smell the snow to come. They reached the top and Clegg scanned the moor for his sheep. From where he stood, the land dipped and rolled away down to Stannon Marsh, a sea of dun, shading to brown, and back to dun again, littered with granite and brooded over by the mass of Cragg Tor.

A movement on the edge of the marsh made him start forward. White dots crossed and re-crossed the dark brown heather, came together and parted again, purposeful movement too rapid for sheep. A horseman appeared round a boulder, and then another. There came a glimpse of a red coat and Clegg realised he was watching the hunt. He called Skipper to heel and watched the distant line of riders move slowly towards the marsh, then with a word to the dog, he turned to follow the ridge towards Cragg Tor.

The rain hissed through the brown-tipped rushes of Stannon Marsh, where a solitary gnarled hawthorn creaked and groaned so that the dog fox lying in the hollow beneath its roots started up several times in alarm. He was in his first winter, yet the long guard hairs of his coat had grown almost white so that his pelt was grey. It was the time of the shortest days and he slept lightly as the lowering cloud diminished the already dwindling light. Half-asleep, he listened to the wind and the creaking tree. As daylight waned, the air became colder so that he moved frequently and curled his brush more tightly over his nose. It was during one of his wakeful moments that he heard sounds other than the wind in the thorn, but the noise, faint and distorted, was downwind and he was not sure of its direction or even if he had heard it at all. For several moments, he lay still, ears pricked, listening, tense, but the sound did not come again and gradually he relaxed into a dose.

Beyond the marsh, the ground rose steeply to the rugged outline of Cragg Tor, its topmost boulders hidden in mist. A single red-coated horseman stood below the tor, his grey mount fidgeting in the cold rain. Josh Huccaby studied his hounds as they worked slowly through the dead tussock grass on the edge of the marsh. He looked at his watch. It was half past three. In the last half-hour, the temperature had dropped, which to Josh meant two things: the likelihood of a good scent, and the certainty of snow. He turned to glance at a small group of riders huddled in the shelter of a boulder fifty yards behind him. Not more than half a dozen left, he thought, and they look ready to call it a day. A cold trickle of water seeped through his sodden stock and ran down between his shoulder blades. He shivered and turned his attention once more to his hounds.

Josh had been Master and huntsman for nearly twenty years. Hunting was his life and farming his livelihood, and both had kept him lean and hard so that at fifty he felt the cold and wet less than most men half his age. Nevertheless, weather like this played havoc with his rheumatism and he thought longingly of the blazing fire and hot bath that awaited him in the big stone farmhouse of Menaridden. For once, Josh hoped that the marsh would draw a blank so that he could finish the day there.

A white bitch shook herself in front of his horse's nose and looked up expectantly. "Get on, Melody, Lieu on there!" He waved his horn in the direction of the marsh. "Go'rn, old girl, fetch 'im out!" The bitch turned to join the rest of the pack drawing through the rushes.

There was a spatter of hoof beats as Tom Slade, the young whipper-in, urged his chestnut mare down a steep slope past the sheltering riders. Two bedraggled hounds followed close at his mare's heels. "Found 'em in Harrison's kale!" he called as he squelched passed Josh at a tired canter.

The Master nodded and the whip rode on to the far end of the marsh. Tom pulled up at a cluster of grey boulders. Here he turned the chestnut's tail to the wind and sat hunched in the saddle to watch for the first signs of movement that would indicate a fox on the move. He was secretly pleased that the hounds had drawn through most of the marsh without so much as a whimper, for if this were blank the boss would surely call it a day, and there was a Young Farmers' Club dance that evening which he might get to if they finished by four o'clock.

The fox woke with a start at the sound of hoof beats. As the whip moved upwind, he caught the scent of horse and man, and he knew enough to associate it with his main enemy: the pack. The fox had been hunted before. He had learned the signs when as a cub he had been chased from the same marsh. Then, the pack had consisted of young untried hounds equally as inexperienced as himself. They had learned to hunt as he had learned to flee, and now they were seasoned veterans: steady unwavering dog-hounds that could hold on to the slightest hint of scent, and with them the bitches, fast and murderous. There were eighteen couple quartering the marsh towards the thorn tree; thirty-six mud-spattered, white, tan and black shapes working backwards and forwards, noses pressed to the sodden earth, seeking the scent that would make their hackles rise and cause them to cry out in fury. The fox waited only long enough to make sure of the position of the horseman, then he left the thorn tree and ran quickly towards the high ground away from him.

Tom saw the shape slip out from under the thorn and watched the fox as it twisted through the tussocks and up the slope towards Cragg Tor, then, not taking his eyes off it, he raised his black hunting cap and waved it in the air. At the same moment, the leading hounds caught their first taste of scent, making them whimper with excitement. The whimper became a clamour and within half a minute, thirty-six hounds were strung out in a line, giving tongue to the collective fury of the pack.

The fox heard the cry as he turned uphill and headed into the wind towards an earth on Cragg Tor. He threaded between the boulders, flattening his ears as the sleet turned to snow. At the base of the tor, he stopped to listen. The deep bay of a dog-hound told him what he wanted to know and he shook the snow from his coat and ran on round a large boulder shaped like a giant fist, where he felt the wind ease and at the same time caught the sickly scent of man.

Beyond Fist Rock and just in front of the earth was a man with a dog. He did not move, neither did he make a sound, and for several seconds, fox and man stared at each other until the fox turned and headed on round the tor. Clegg held Skipper's nape and watched him go.

Now the fox ran with the wind behind him. He crossed a brook that ran into Stannon Marsh, then doubled back to run down the stony channel carved out by its swift waters. Where the brook emptied into the marsh, he stopped to flop, belly down, in a pool among the rushes, letting his tongue feel the ice-cold water, then once more came the sound of the hounds and he was up with a quick shake and off across the marsh.

The hounds had stopped below the earth on Cragg Tor, baffled by the scent left by the collie. A few went to bay round the entrance where the old scent of fox still clung to the lichen-covered rocks, but within seconds a pied bitch had found the line running downhill and the pack was once more in full cry through the thickening snow.

They checked again at the brook, for scent does not hold in running water. They overshot the line where the fox had doubled back, but Josh, knowing the ways of foxes, had 'lifted' them and taken them down towards the marsh where Melody gave tongue once more.

The fox heard Melody's deep throaty cry and increased his speed along the sheep track which crossed firmer ground. The turf was short and springy and with the wind behind him, he held his own up the steep side of Stannon Down. At the top, he could hear nothing but the howling wind which sent flurries of twisting snow after him. Where the ground began to slope downwards, he suddenly changed direction to the left and ran down a stony gully which led to a narrow road. At the verge, he stopped to ease his lungs and listen. The whining discord of the pack seemed far distant and then was lost. He crossed the road and into a gorse brake. The gorse was thick and dry underneath and he crept into its welcome dimness.

The pied bitch, Victress, led the pack over Stannon Down, and behind her came Melody, then a black and tan dog called Tarquin. Fifty yards behind them, the rest of the pack stretched out in a long line to the marsh. Victress ran mute, growling murder under her breath. Powerful and fast, she had brought sudden death to more than a score of foxes in two seasons' hunting. Her speed took her past the place where the fox had turned down the gully. Melody and Tarquin followed, and soon the three leading hounds had lost the scent.

It was an old tan hound with long black ears who found it again. Old Warrior was slow compared to the younger hounds, but his nose was infallible and he rarely overran a line. His deep-bellied voice brought the rest of the pack to him just as Tom reached the top of Stannon Down.

The fox had gained less than a minute by the delay at the gully but it gave him the chance to get his second wind. He left the gorse brake when Warrior gave tongue and pushed his way through the dead bracken that covered a gradual slope up to a drystone wall. A single leap took him on top where he paused to hear Warrior's voice booming out down by the road.

In the gathering gloom, Tom could just see the fox outlined against the whitening fields. "He's off for Trenden Wood for a pound!" he called back excitedly. "And it's a grey 'un!" he added, all thoughts of the dance now gone. But Josh merely hunched his shoulders still more and dug his heels into his sweating horse.

The fox dropped off the wall and ran quickly up a small grass field through a well-worn hole in the hedge and down the hill on the far side. This was familiar country and he followed a frequently used route to one of his favourite hunting places: Trenden Wood. It was nearly all downhill over short turf, but he was beginning to tire and already the leading hounds had scrambled over the wall. They sounded closer and he realised they were gaining.

Three more fields, over another road and it was uphill again. Only one more field now to Trenden Wood, but it was ploughed ready for spring barley and the recent rain had turned it to mud. He found a deep furrow where the snow had melted to slush in the brown water. The mud clung to his coat and seemed to double the weight of his brush. Now he could smell the hound behind, a hound that ran mute. In front was a ditch with a culvert leading into the wood. As the fox dropped into the ditch, Victress fell on top of him, but the hound was off balance and the fox managed to squeeze through the culvert as the hound's teeth snatched a mouthful of muddy hair from his brush.

The wood was surrounded by a bank topped with a hedge and two strands of barbed wire. By the time Victress had scrambled out of the ditch, up the bank and through the hedge, the fox was fifty yards into the wood, making for a thicket of bramble and blackthorn. He crawled inside, aching and footsore. There was a sharp pain in his lungs and as he lay, he began to stiffen. He knew that he must move before every muscle in his body knotted in cramp and movement became impossible.

Victress followed the line into the wood but it was Warrior who traced the scent through a maze of rabbit paths to the thicket. Once more, his voice summoned the pack and soon the hounds were crowded down one side, howling at the fresh scent of fox which seeped through the thorny entanglement. Tarquin began pushing his way along the rabbit run that the fox had followed through the brambles. He stopped with a yelp as he met a barrier of blackthorn, but his litter mate, Tipster, was close behind and Tarquin was forced to push on. The fox could hear them coming and knew that sooner or later one of them would burst through, so he realised he must move again.

Trenden Wood was the furthest point of the young fox's territory. Beyond was strange country where he knew no sanctuaries and no sure paths, but he must move or die. Slowly, he crept out of the thicket away from the hounds, bracing his stiffening joints for a last bid to return the way he had come. The thicket was too big for the pack to encircle and he was able to reach the edge of a broad ride which ran the length of the wood. He turned left, the way back to the moor, then stopped suddenly, for the whip and the chestnut mare stood dark against the fresh fall of snow. The fox hesitated a moment, then turned and ran for the gate at the other end of the ride. The whip's shrill, "Tayouw!" echoed behind him as the quick notes of the horn gathered the pack.

The tired fox squeezed under the bottom rail of the gate and found himself in a narrow lane bounded by high banks. He turned right and ran up the centre of the tarmac, leaving a single line of footprints in the thin sprinkling of snow, then abruptly he turned left and up the bank as Victress led the pack out of the wood and into the lane. The grey shape dropped on to a grass field and loped wearily towards a flock of Longwool sheep huddled against a hedge for shelter. They moved uneasily at his approach, then scattered as he ran in amongst them. Beyond the sheep, he wriggled through a hurdle set in a gap in the hedge, then out on to an open expanse of whitening pasture.

The pack checked, confused by the acrid scent of sheep, but Josh took them on to the clearly visible line of footprints leading to the hurdle and, jumping it in a single stride, was just in time to see a small dark form, outlined against the snow trotting towards a line of trees on the horizon.

It was nearly dark and the hounds laboured through deepening drifts in silence save for the occasional growl and snort as breath was expelled from overworked lungs. They ran mechanically, an ever-changing pattern of white, black and tan; a thousand years of breeding ensuring that they would stick to the line until the scent failed or until they, like their quarry, dropped with muscle fatigue and exhaustion. Two splashes of scarlet, their outlines blurred with snow, followed on tired horses. Neither man spoke, each concentrating on the effort of staying with the hounds at all costs.

The fox knew that he was nearing the end of his endurance. He could sense the pack drawing near, their amber eyes fixed on a spot at the nape of his neck where the fatal bite would come. The sensation made him exert the stiffening muscles in his loins so that he made a last desperate leap through a rusty barbed wire fence into the dark blur of a blackthorn clump. Immediately he found himself falling, then his pads touched loose stone and he half-fell and half-slid down a near-vertical slope. Small stones skittered down in front of him and almost immediately larger pieces of rock showered from above, then something brown and heavy landed beside him with a yelp. Warrior, unable to check his final lunge, had fallen headlong over the precipice. Both animals tumbled down the loose screed together, but the fox gained his feet as they reached the bottom and scrambled into the cover of some large boulders, while the tan hound lay still.

They had fallen down the sheer face of the disused quarry that men had cut into the side of Ravenscoombe, to take the rust-coloured stone at the time when the great oaks that grew along the rim were saplings, newly planted to provide bark for tanning and wood for the charcoal burners. The quarry was long and narrow, its sloping sides covered by a dense growth of elm and sycamore with many clumps of bramble where the tree canopy thinned.

The fox lay under a rock, deafened by the noise of rushing water, straining to hear from the pack above. He looked up to where a stream cascaded over the quarry's edge. The thin film of vapour that hung over the water outlined a pied hound's head and shoulders, and a moment later Victress plunged down the waterfall into the pool beneath.

The fox started off down the track that ran along the floor of the quarry as Victress clambered out of the water. He heard the flap of ears and jowl as she shook herself, then the pied hound feathered through the snow--covered rocks, gulped the scent of the fox and ran silently on the line. Tarquin slid down through the sycamores to give tongue on the track below. Tipster followed, then Rowdy and Melody, and more hounds tumbled, slid and scrambled down the sloping sides as the tired fox loped wearily fifty paces ahead of them. Victress gave a single growl of triumph behind him, and stretched for the final bite as the fox suddenly turned into a clump of brambles and disappeared down one of the many openings to a large badger sett.

The Master and whipper-in skirted the quarry to enter the coombe by a cart way through Ravenscoombe Farm. When they reached the sett, half the pack were milling round the hole. Tarquin howled mournfully to 'mark' where the fox had gone to ground. Victress had already enlarged the opening enough to get her head and shoulders in and several more hounds were scratching at other openings. Josh drew out his horn and blew a long blast while the whip called the hounds, "Come away, Rowdy! Leave it, Tarquin!"

One by one, they turned and gathered round the Master's horse. Josh counted them, then blew on his horn again and more hounds appeared, steaming as the snow evaporated on their hot flanks, tongues lolling. In ones and twos, they appeared out of the semi-darkness, and again they were counted, in pairs. "Seventeen couple, seventeen and a half ... "

The Master dismounted and walked back into the quarry, calling the missing hound by name. He followed hound prints to the foot of the quarry face and found the snow-covered body of his tan hound. Dropping to his knees, he lifted the old dog's head until the black muzzle was close to his cheek. There was a faint hint of warm breath. He lifted Warrior and carried him in his arms back to where the whip held his horse. Tom took the hound and cradled him over the front of his saddle with an inquiring look at Josh. The Master nodded. "He's got a nasty knock on the head, but he's alive, thank heavens. Let's get 'em home," and to the hounds, "Come along, then, coo-up, coo-up." They fell in at his horse's heels, heads up, sterns erect. It was the end of the day.

CHAPTER 2

THE HUNTERS rode in silence save for the steady crunch of hooves on crisp snow. The sky had cleared and a crescent moon slid out from behind the last wisp of cloud. A grey vapour of warm breath brooded over the pack and threads of hoar frost hung white from whisker and tail. They followed the old track through a thick tangle of blackthorn and bramble and into the dimness of Colspit Wood. Below them, the glint of water showed where the stream from Ravenscoombe slowed through soggy water meadows to join the River Asher.

Out of the wood, they crossed the river by an ancient stone clapper bridge where the ivy-covered ruins of a watermill stood: a silent witness to bygone prosperity. As they passed, a barn owl wheezed and coughed its last snore of the day, then launched itself noiselessly from the rotten beams to hunt the riverbank. The bird swooped low over the water and surprised an otter as it scuffed through the reeds. The animal gave a shrill whistle and disappeared below the water with a dull plop. Josh heard the sound and knew its meaning. He spoke to his hounds and whistled through his teeth lest the younger ones' riot after the water wanderer.

The track wound up past the gate to Ravenscoombe Farm. Josh stopped and considered for a moment, then, seeing a light through the half-door of the shippon, he dismounted and walked stiffly over to seek the occupant. He pushed open the bottom door and stood silhouetted, broad-shouldered and bow-legged, against the soft yellow light. The familiar warm smell of fresh cow dung enveloped him, and a hurricane lamp threw deep flitting shadows round the six South Devon cows tied in standing; five of the cows suckled calves while the sixth was being milked by a bearded man, his head buried in the cow's flank, duffle-coated shoulders working rhythmically to the chip-chip-chip of milk squirted into a metal bucket.

Josh had never met the owner of Ravenscoombe but he knew from the descriptions of local gossips that this must be the man. Apparently, he had not heard him come in, or if he had he showed no sign of it for the chip-chip-chip continued and the head pushed deeper into the cow's flank.

Josh cleared his throat. "Sorry to trouble you ... er ... Mr Granger, isn't it?" he said in his gruff voice.

The mop of black hair turned slowly, and a pair of deep-set grey eyes looked at him. For several seconds, the chip-chip-chip continued, then gradually the back straightened and Clegg stood up, bucket in one hand and stool in the other. "That's me," he said quietly, putting the bucket in the corner and turning to face the scarlet-coated man. He was taller and younger than Josh had anticipated from the tales he had heard in Ashton Market.

Josh cleared his throat again. "Would you mind giving us a hand…?" He paused as the grey eyes receded into a frown. "We've got an injured hound. I'll want to put him somewhere until we can collect him in the Land Rover."

Clegg studied the speaker for several seconds, unable to mask his resentment at the intrusion, yet wanting to help a stricken animal.

"You can put him in the loft." He took down the lantern and led the way out and round the shippon which was built into the side of the hill so that the door to the top storey was at ground level. The loft was piled with hay on one side and a few bales of straw on the other. He nodded towards the straw. "He'll be all right there."

While the Master and whipper-in carried the hound into the loft, Clegg fetched a bowl of water and some scraps from the kitchen. By the time he returned, Tom was supporting Warrior as he tried to stand, but the dog whimpered with pain so they eased him back on to the straw. He raised his head, the black ears moved, and a mud-spattered tail thumped the floor, then the hound stretched out and lay still.

No one spoke until eventually Josh said, "Come over the old quarry face in Colspit … " He felt some explanation was necessary even if it were not asked for. " … reckon his ribs are knocked about," he continued.

Clegg nodded and ended the one-sided conversation by turning to lead the way out.

In the yard, Josh turned and held out his large gnarled hand. "Well, I'm much obliged to you, Mr Granger," he said as brightly as he knew how. "We'll collect him as soon as possible." The hand was grasped without enthusiasm.

They walked towards the gate as large white flakes began falling again. Josh brushed them off his sleeve, screwing up his face as they settled on nose and eyebrows. He pointed upwards with his crop. "If we get much more of this, I can't see us getting to you before tomorrow morning. Hope that'll be all right." He raised his black hunting cap, more out of habit than politeness. "Many thanks again." Then, turning to the whip, "Right, Tom, let's be off."

The two men walked to where the horses stood. "A queer fish, that, sir," said Tom as he put his foot in the stirrup.

Josh hauled himself on to the grey. "Oh, I don't know," he said pensively. "Just because a chap doesn't jaw the hind leg off a donkey doesn't mean to say he's peculiar. Some men are just made that way."

"If you ask me," retorted the whip, "he's got something to hide."

"Well, no one is asking you, m'lad, so let's get on home. Come up, m'beauties! Come along, then!" Josh called up his hounds and, head bent into the oncoming snow, led them towards the track which led up to the Ashton road.

Clegg watched them go and the tension that had been building up gradually eased. "I don't know what's the matter with you these days," he said out loud. "Those two were harmless enough. That chap - the Master or whatever he was - did his best to be polite. You might at least have tried to make conversation." He shrugged his shoulders. Talking to himself was becoming a habit.

He went into the shippon, poured some of the milk into an old basin and returned with it to the loft. The hound lifted his head expectantly as the man approached. Clegg squatted down and pushed the basin under the dog's nose. "Well, old feller, what have you been up to?" His voice had a quiet, husky tone that seemed to have a calming effect on all animals and caused the hound's tail to thump on the floor. "Come on, drink up." The large pink tongue lapped, slowly at first, then with increasing interest until the milk was gone and the bowl licked clean. "That's better." Clegg stroked the tan head and gently pulled one black ear. "You'll be fine by the morning."

He finished the rest of the chores as quickly as possible, taking special care to shut in his dozen Rhode Islands, for a deep snow meant the foxes would be hungry. The final job was to look at the gathered sheep for signs of any that might be ready to lamb. They were not easy to pick out through the falling snow and Clegg had to search the length of the sheltering hedge bank before he found them. Counting was impossible, so he walked round the flock to look for any that had separated themselves, a sure sign of something amiss. A small dark patch moved against the white background about twenty yards from the sheep, and as he walked towards it, Clegg saw that it was one of the dozen or so Scotch Blackface ewes in the flock. She lay, head erect, tense, and as he approached she got up to face him, her tail twitching nervously. He could see she was heavy, but he had to catch her and if she was about to lamb, he would have to get her inside.

"This is where a steady dog comes in handy," he told the ewe. He said much more to her as he and Skipper gently worked her towards the corner of the field nearest the flock. She went readily into a bunch of three old matrons who held their ground so that he was able to make a quick grab at the Blackface's fleece. There was a struggle. "Thank heavens your sort have got horns!" he gasped as he took hold of one and held it firmly while the ewe bucked and snorted in her attempts to break away.

With one hand holding the horn and the other clutching a handful of fleece above the tail, Clegg half-dragged, half-pushed the reluctant animal towards the field gate. Once out of the gate and away from the others, he was able to drive the ewe into the yard and entice it into a loose box next to the Dartmoor ewe and her lamb. He fetched the lantern and felt the ewe's abdomen and swelling udder. Yes, she would lamb before morning. He gave her a handful of crushed oats, waited until she had settled to feed and, after a final look at the ewe and lamb next door, made his way to the farmhouse, a warm fire and supper.

It was nearly midnight by the time the washing-up was finished, and Skipper had been given his one full meal of the day. For a few minutes, Clegg sat by the fire reading a two-week-old *Farmer's Weekly*. The hissing pressure lamp threw greenish patterns on the uneven whiteness of walls and ceiling, and the last piece of coal flickered and reddened into embers. His head nodded twice, then with a snort he wrenched himself from sleep, put out the lamp and climbed the narrow creaking stairs in the dark.

As always, before getting into bed he stood for several minutes gazing out of the uncurtained window which overlooked the farm buildings and surrounding fields. The snow shower had passed, and he could see the sheep huddled together under the hedge bank, white encrusted hummocks with the haze of cooling breath hanging over them like faint wisps of smoke. Instinctively, he looked at the stars to seek old friends, Orion, the Plough, the Pole Star. They really do twinkle, he thought, and memories of night passages in *Seadrift* came back, but he shut them out and concentrated on finding the familiar constellations.

Just above the horizon, the thin sliver of moon hung on its back over a smooth icing-sugar world where there was no good pasture or bad, no bracken and uneaten tussocks, only a gentle whiteness etched by the wavering black line of the stream. He opened the window and breathed the cold air, rejoicing in the silence of this hard, beautiful place that was his.

He was in bed when Warrior's howl made him sit up with a jerk. "Damn the dog!" he said aloud. "Damn them both!" he repeated as Skipper joined in from his bed in the scullery. The noise stopped as suddenly as it had begun, but not for long, and the ensuing barking reached a crescendo as Clegg pulled on trousers and sweater over the top of his pyjamas. Grabbing his duffle coat from the back of the kitchen door, he slipped on his boots, picked up a big torch and went out.

"Shut up, you bloody old fool!' he bawled as he ran across the yard towards the shippon. The baying was frantic, and he was about to unbolt the loft door when the bleating of the ewes on the other side of the yard caught his attention. "Now what?" he murmured and, changing his mind, hurried over to the loose- boxes. The torch showed the Dartmoor ewe at the far end of the box, stamping one forefoot and calling wildly. Of the lamb there was no sign, nor was any needed for the whole place stank of fox and a freshly gnawed hole in one of the rotten door planks had grey hairs caught in its rough edges.

"Damn!" Clegg closed his eyes and slammed the doors. "Why the hell can't something go right just for once?" He kicked out at an old bucket and sent it flying across the snow.

The dogs stopped barking. One by one, the stars were obliterated and it began to snow again.

CHAPTER 3

THE GREY FOX squeezed under the gate as a shaft of light from the torch swung across the yard. He paused to listen as the baying stopped and the scent of man faded with the receding crunch of footsteps, then he jerked his head to get a better grip of the lamb in his mouth and trotted off along the sheltered side of the hedge bank past the sleeping sheep. The ewes stirred uneasily as the shadow slid by. One stood up and snorted but the fox was gone, leaving his pungent smell to trouble the flock long after.

He ate the lamb by the stream where the rushes bristled through shallow drifts and the toothed outline of a broken alder gave just enough cover. The hunt from Cragg Tor had sharpened his appetite and he gulped the lamb down quickly, licking the tiny ringlets of wool from his snout. He lapped ice-cold water from a still pool, crouching cat-like in the soft snow, then, stretching his weary limbs one after another, he trotted uphill towards the head of the coombe.

Between moor and coombe, he hunted the rabbit runs where the wind had swept the short turf clear of snow, finding only stale scents and frozen droppings. He reached the skyline at a lope and ran across the Ashton road, floundering through the deep drifts on his belly. On the far side, he rolled and shook himself before trotting briskly along the roadside verge, licking at the snow to cool his lolling tongue. Past the granite gatepost where the steep winding track led down to Ravenscoombe Farm, he went on to where a cattle grid ridged the smoothness of the road, then turning into the shadows, he jumped a low stone wall into a small copse. Here he paused, for beyond the trees an untidy jumble of tin sheds and old vehicles barred the way.

The fox squatted in the darkness and savoured the air, identifying the various scents and listening for his only enemies: man and dog. No warning sounds came, and he crept closer, nose to wind, following a faint warm smell that quickened his saliva and reminded him that he was still hungry. Beyond the tin sheds, an old railway van stood in a small paddock surrounded by bowls and feeding troughs, and from that van came the smell and contented wheezings of poultry.

The fox stalked slowly round the van, sniffing the boards, seeking a place where the warm air came through, a place to push in his long snout.

He found it in a corner where contact with the damp earth had rotted the bottom boards, and he began to gnaw.

A rat darted out and across to the sheds, leaving a long tail groove in the snow, but the fox paid no heed, intent on tearing the rotten wood. As the hole grew larger, the hens clucked nervously, shuffling on their perches and peering down to where the cold air brought in the smell to be feared. The mouldering floorboards gave and the fox squeezed through into the moist warmth of the van. Quickly, he pulled a Leghorn from her perch and bit through her neck before she could cackle, but the fluttering wings panicked the rest and he was met by a squawking, beating mass. In the confined space, he too panicked, biting and clawing, until the sound of a terrier barking made him snatch the nearest body and drag it through the hole just as Tacky Bowden emerged from his cottage, carrying an ancient single-barrel twelve-bore. He shone his torch in time to see the grey fox dart through the tangle of old iron. The shot cracked in the still night and pellets rattled through the rusty metal, but the fox kept running with the hen firmly clamped between his jaws.

Tacky counted four bodies and two more hens badly mauled. He pushed a large stone into the hole in the boards, then called his terrier which had bounded into the copse in pursuit of the fox. "Yer, Tiger! Yer, boy!" He cursed the dog when it failed to obey, muttering to himself, "Damn dog, damn bloody fox. Us'll know 'e again, danged if us won't. A grey 'un 'e were for certain. Us'll know 'e again." He tapped the barrel of the shot gun and called Tiger once more before stumping up the steps to his back door.

The fox ate half the hen and left the rest in the corner of a field next to the larch plantation. He marked the nearest tree with his own scent from the glands at the root of his tail and repeated the act on the corner stone of the mill ruin. By the badger sett, he marked the ground again and in the lattice work of shadows lay back his ears and screamed into the night. He listened for an answering call and once more screamed, but no answer came. He tasted the air, shook the wet from his coat and entered the sett, confident that the coombe was his.

It was the hour when cold bites deepest, the no man's land in time between the creatures of the night and those of the day. In his ivy-covered niche, the barn owl spewed his mouse pellets, puffed out his feathers and settled to sleep. The hounds at Menaridden stirred on their benches, pushing chilled noses further into warm flanks.

Clegg Granger grouped for the eiderdown and waited, cold and half-conscious, for the alarm to go off. The jangle dragged him back from the sanctuary of oblivion to face the reality of the day. As always on waking, his first thoughts were of the house by the sea, of Cathy and the warm feel of her next to him. He pushed the images away and, with an effort, thought of the day's work ahead: how deep the drifts would be, whether or not the fox had returned for the other ewe's lamb, if indeed she had lambed. He made a mental list of the jobs to do, jobs that would fill every waking moment until weariness eased him once again into sleep and the hope of oblivion.

He dressed quickly, shivering until the thick seaman's sweater captured his body warmth. He scraped the opaque film of ice from the inside of one of the leaded window panes and looked out. It was still dark, and the stars had gone. The sides of the coombe were smooth and white.

"Good for tobogganing. Dad, let's get the sledge." The child's voice seared his memory and he shut his eyes and concentrated again on the work ahead.

Clegg vowed no more early lambing as he faced the icy blast outside the back door and his wellingtons sank into a foot of snow. He trudged over to the loose boxes and shone his torch in. Sure enough, the Blackface ewe had lambed and was licking the wet grey mite at her feet. She moved uneasily as the beam swung across the trampled straw, then she looked back at her flanks and lay down, only to get up immediately and go to her lamb.

"You're not quite right, are you, old lady?" Clegg talked to the ewe as he entered the box and, with arms outstretched, drove her into the corner. She eyed him wildly, but he quickly had a handful of fleece and in a single smooth movement had her on her side and pinned under one knee while his right hand felt her abdomen. "Steady now." The ewe stopped struggling. "That's better. I'm not going to hurt you." A look of mild surprise came over his face and he let the ewe go. "We'll keep an eye on you for a little while, just in case."

Twenty minutes later, the ewe was still uncomfortable, although her lamb was up and sucking heartily. Clegg went to the house and returned with a bucket of hot water, soap and towel which he placed in one corner. He caught her as before and lay her down beside the bucket, and when she lay quiet he quickly washed his hands, leaving plenty of soap on the right one, then very gently he felt into the uterus, his first and second fingers feeling carefully into the womb. Could he feel a foot? Or was it a head? Or, worse still, was it the soft wetness of a body across the womb? He closed his eyes in concentration. No, it wasn't a breach, there was the hard spikiness of a foot. He breathed a sigh of relief and opened his eyes. And there was the other foot, but no head between. A head twisted back meant a difficult lambing and almost certainly a dead lamb. He closed his eyes and felt again. A tail, that was it! The lamb was coming backwards. He withdrew his hand and let the ewe get up. "Not too bad, old girl. It'll take a little time, but we'll have another look in a quarter of an hour."

Ten minutes later, she was straining hard and Clegg washed again and felt into her. This time, he could hold the tiny slippery feet between his fingers and as the ewe strained, he pulled until, with a grunt from the ewe, the lamb was born. He watched as the ewe licked the lamb, cleaning it and massaging life into the tiny veins. As soon as it struggled to its feet, he gently put its black nose to the mother's teat which it immediately took in its mouth and hung on like a limpet, sucking the nutritious colostrum so necessary for its survival. Clegg closed the loose box door, satisfied, if not pleased. It was unusual for him to get twins so early and from a Blackface. It made up for the loss in the night. He looked over the coombe to where the greyness of dawn made Colspit Wood stand out black against snow and sky. "One to you and two to me!" he muttered.

Dawn brought up dark snow clouds out of the north-west and the first flurries of the day. The wind ruffled the feathers of a hen buzzard where she roosted in a hollow cleft of an oak, her eyes fixed on a dark speck by the larches, a speck she had watched since before first light. She spread her broad ragged wings and planed down on to the remains of the grey fox's kill and tore at the ribs with her curved beak. A pair of magpies alighted in a nearby hawthorn, chakkering at the large but timid hawk until they swept down to drive her away. A crow stalked furtively round the pied birds, snatching a beakful when he could, while the buzzard hung in the air above, mewing plaintively at her loss. Suddenly, she wheeled and was gone, and the magpies stopped feeding and listened, their long iridescent tails cocking up and down as they balanced on the carcass. The crow had disappeared. High above, a large black bird arched its wings and circled lower, calling his deep guttural "kronk!". The magpies fluttered back to the hawthorn with short hasty wing beats, there to sit silently as the raven swooped to claim the prize, alighting a yard from it and jabbing his long, murderous beak in the air several times as a warning to those who might contemplate interference.

The hen buzzard did not wait to watch the raven, but caught an upcurrent and flew high over the ridge to the Ashton road, over Tacky Bowden's thatched roof and down into the next broad valley where the fat ewes of Menaridden were being fed in long troughs by a leather-jacketed youth with a blue tractor. She sat on the top of an electricity pole, waiting for the sheep to finish so that she could scavenge any of the small cubes of meal left by the animals.

From where he stood at the tall bay window of Menaridden House, Josh Huccaby watched the large brown bird puff her feathers against the cold. He saw the grey clouds gathering and contemplated the prospects of deep snow, with no hunting and horses to keep exercised and fit. Hay and cattle food would be used at twice the normal rate to keep the out-wintered stock going, not to mention the likelihood of being cut off if the Ashton road became blocked.

"No chance of fetching old Warrior in this lot" he said to his wife who sat at the far end of the room finishing her breakfast. She ignored the remark, and Josh stirred his tea without looking around. "Did I tell you we found a grey fox yesterday? Haven't seen one like it since just after the war. You remember, when they lost some from that fur farm over by Lamerford? A fair old run he gave us too: Cragg Tor to Trenden, then on to - "

"How often have I asked you not to wear those filthy trousers in the dining room?" Isobel Huccaby's voice cut across his words and he looked down at the baggy cords stained with horse's sweat and contemplated the toes of his pale blue socks which peeped conspicuously through the holes in his old grey stockings. His face was expressionless as he carefully placed his empty cup on the table and left the room.

The back door slammed as he went out, shouting for Tom. The buzzard lifted her wings and once more drifted up to beat steadily towards Trenden Wood where she knew the rabbits would be foraging the snow-free ground beneath the spruces. Slowly and methodically, she hunted the woodland edge until a movement where white snow met brown earth caused her to plummet and zigzag through the straight trunks to soar up in a shower of snow and spruce needles, clutching the limp body of a half-grown rabbit in her yellow talons.

She carried it over the fields where the ewes pawed the snow to get at the tufts of coarse grass underneath, grass that they had disdained to eat all through the summer and autumn. Two wing beats took her over the old quarry and two more planed her into the topmost fork of the tallest elm. She laid the rabbit in the broad cleft and, placing one foot on its head, tore open the soft belly with her curved beak and gulped down the warm entrails.

She ate her fill, leaving the remnants for the crows to pick, then she dropped on to a lower branch out of the wind and dozed. A twig snapped far down the wood and the buzzard opened one eye. She shifted uneasily and cocked her head to one side, listening. The steady crunch of two legs in snow came closer. Two legs meant man, and man was not to be trusted. The bird shook herself awake and watched until the bent figure came into view, then she launched herself into the air once more, mewing her annoyance at the intruder as she flew away.

Tacky Bowden was too intent on studying the ground to notice the flight of the buzzard. With Tiger straining at the end of a long piece of string, he was seeking the tracks of the grey fox. Tacky had found the place where it had floundered through the drifts and discovered the single line of pad marks across the field before the fresh falls of snow had covered them. By the larches, he saw the remains of his black Leghorn hen and it confirmed his guess that the chicken thief was lying up in Colspit Wood. Inside the wood, the tracks were difficult to follow, but Tacky knew the place from his boyhood days and remembered the old sett where the badger diggers from Ashton used to pit their terriers against the brocks and he guessed that here would be an ideal place for 'Charlie' to lay low.

Tiger made straight for the large hole, almost dragging the old man off his feet. "Steady, y' damned ol' fool!"

The terrier yapped excitedly at the entrance to the sett as Tacky, puffing and wheezing, snatched at the string and climbed up behind his dog. He dropped on all fours to get his head as close as possible to the ground, and sure enough, among the musty smells of earth and leaves, the pungent stink of fox drifted up from the depths of the hold. He grunted with satisfaction and, pulling the furious Tiger away, tied him to a nearby sapling. He unslung a large poacher's bag from his shoulders and took out a small folding spade, a bundle of newspapers and a plastic bag containing a piece of raw mutton. He took the spade and papers and searched around the sett for the emergency bolt holes which the past occupants were certain to have provided. He found two higher up the slope and these he stuffed with the paper, ramming it well home and finally covering the holes with soil and stones. The exertion made him sweat and he paused to mop his reddening face and look up at the sky, calculating how long it might be before the next fall of snow. Satisfied with his work, he returned to the main entrance and took from the inside pocket of his tattered brown overcoat a stout peg, attached to which was a length of cord and a loop of thin brass wire. It was a poacher's snare, more deadly than the illegal gin trap in the hands of an expert, which Tacky was.

He cut a short stick, made a split in one end, sharpening the other, and pushed it into the soil about two inches from the hole, then he pressed the static end of the running loop into the split so that the wire was held at a hand's breadth above the ground, with the loop just large enough for a fox's head to go through. The snare was secured by hammering a peg into the bank with a large stone. He took out the piece of mutton, which was to have been Tiger's dinner, and cut off a sliver of fat which he used to grease the wire to make it run easily and also to help mask his scent. Finally, he placed the raw meat a yard in front of the snare and pinned it there with another sharpened stick.

Tacky straightened up and surveyed the trap. "Nearly done," he said to himself and opened a separate pocket at the back of his bag. From it, he took the cream wing of a barn owl, and with its soft pinions, carefully brushed the snow smooth round the entrance to the sett. "There, a proper job," he said with satisfaction.

When it came to poaching, Tacky was a craftsman, and it pleased him to see a job well done. He did not hate the fox; in fact, he had no feelings towards it at all, except that it had taken his property and would do so again unless he killed it.

The old man untied the terrier, picked up his bag and spade, and carefully made his way down to the track. "All us wants now," he said to the dog, "is a nice little sprinklin' o' snow." Even as he spoke, the first flakes sifted through the topmost branches of the elm tree.

CHAPTER 4

AS HE TRUDGED homewards, Tacky pondered whether he should go and tell the new owner of the quarry that he had set a wire for the fox on his property. He had met Clegg only once, when the farm was auctioned, and he had no idea what his reaction to someone snaring foxes on his land might be. He could be a keen fox hunter. He knew Clegg did not ride, for there were no horses on the farm, but he could be a foot follower, in which case the interview would be very unpleasant and would certainly end in his having to remove his morning's work. On the other hand, the man was from upcountry and rumour had it that he had come from the town, in which case he could well be anti-blood sports. Tacky smiled as he realised the results would be the same, and he decided he was on a loser either way.

He reached the ruined mill and paused to get his breath, still mulling over his course of action. He realised that if he were to catch the perpetrator of the previous night's crime, he would need the full co-operation of the owner of Ravenscoombe. The last thought made him smile wryly, for he still found it difficult to accept that the farm no longer belonged to him as it had done to his father and grandfather. He brushed the snow from one of the granite steps and sat down, and immediately the terrier hopped on to his lap and pushed a wet nose into the old man's grey stubbled cheek.

"Why, I've 'eard Father say that 'is grandfather built this ol' mill." He looked down at the dog and fondled its ears. "Ah, if only yer missus 'adn't been took."

He sighed and pushed the dog away. It was Tacky's custom to blame the loss of his farm on the death of his wife, and to some extent this was true, for she had been the driving force that kept him away from the King's Head, the one who had filled in the Ministry forms, written the letters and kept the books. Without her, Tacky's ramshackle farming could not hold together and he and Ravenscoombe fell to pieces at the same time. Now all he was left with was the cottage and a tiny parcel of land on which to run a few poultry and half a dozen Saddleback sows.

The coldness of the stone penetrated to his buttocks. He put the terrier on the ground and stood up, drawing his breath in sharply and rubbing his backside to restore circulation. It began to snow harder and he sank his scrawny neck further into the upturned collar of his overcoat. He rammed down the sweat-stained grey trilby until there was just enough gap between the brim and the collar for him to see where he was going, then, tightening the piece of baling string that served as a belt, he set off across the clapper bridge towards Ravenscoombe Farm. He had decided to face its new owner.

"The chap will be glad of someone to talk to," he mused, "and 'e's bound to offer a cup of tea, or perhaps even something stronger." The thought strengthened his resolve as he toiled up the track towards the farm.

Clegg was mucking out the shippon when Tacky pushed through the gate into the yard. Tacky could see the bobbing figure through the window where the forkfuls of dung were being thrown out on to a trailer. From the loft came the bark of a dog and Tiger answered it with excited yaps. Tacky eyed the collie when it appeared, hackles raised, in the doorway. He pulled the terrier to him until it strained on its hind legs and finally twisted over backwards with a yelp. The collie took a step forward and a voice from inside growled, "Come here, Skipper." The dog obeyed. Two more forkfuls of dung splattered on to the trailer. There was a pause and then Clegg appeared.

Tacky scooped the terrier into his arms. "Morning, Mr Granger."

Clegg nodded and scraped his boot against the tines of the fork.

"Not much o' weather, is it?" Tacky continued, rubbing the palm of his hand on his coat before holding it out. Clegg frowned as they shook hands. "Us don't see much of one another considering we'm neighbours," Tacky went on, and the frown relaxed.

The fact was that Clegg had not recognised the apparition in the tattered overcoat as the same man he had met at the sale of the farm two years earlier. "Oh yes, Mr Bowden, what can I do for you?"

Tacky put Tiger down but kept the string tight to his side. "Have you lost any lambs lately?" he asked. Clegg raised one eyebrow. "I mean, have you had many taken by foxes?" the old man added quickly.

Clegg nodded. "Well, since you come to mention it, I have."

Tacky gave a long drawn-out "Ah." Then, after a pause, he blurted out with a note of defiance, "Well, I've lost five of my best chickens an' I've set a wire for the varmint along by your old quarry."

He waited for the reply and was visibly relieved when Clegg shrugged his shoulders and turned towards the house.

Tacky followed him to the back door and walked uninvited into the kitchen. Clegg put two mugs on to the table, filled them with hot water from the kettle which was steaming on the hob, and stirred into each a heaped teaspoon of instant coffee. Tacky would have preferred tea but helped himself gladly to sugar and milk and settled down on one side of the table while Clegg seated himself on the other. The old man cupped the steaming mug between his two hands and noisily sipped the hot liquid before re-opening the conversation.

"E's a bold 'un, I can tell 'ee. I seed 'un. A dirt grey fox 'ee were, bold as brass, not ten yards from my back door." The old man paused and took off his battered hat, revealing the sharp line where the weather-beaten red face met the pale baldness of his normally protected dome. A few grey hairs straggled across the bare expanse and he self-consciously stroked them into place as he put the hat on the table.

For the first time, Clegg began to show an interest. "You say it was a grey fox?" he queried. "I didn't think we had such things in this country."

Tacky smiled knowingly. "Nor us, don't normally, but you gets 'em now and again. Why, I've seed black foxes, white, yeller and grey 'uns afore in my lifetime, an' I tell 'ee this, once they get as cheeky as this 'un then watch out, mister. 'E'll be 'aving the dinner off yer plate afore you can say 'knife.'"

"Well, now you come to mention it, I did find some greyish hairs on the bottom of the loose box door last night." Clegg pushed over a tin of biscuits.

"Ah, there, what did I tell 'ee! Took a lamb from inside the buildings, did 'e? And on the same night as 'e 'ad my 'ens. Oh, that's bad, that is. 'E couldn't a bin 'ungry. Just devilment, that's what it were, just devilment." Tacky shook his head and dunked a biscuit in his coffee. He was silent for a few moments, then looked up. "Us'll 'ave to get 'un, Mr Granger, or there'll not be a chicken nor a lamb safe this side of Ashton."

The old man's face glowed with excitement, but Clegg was unmoved by Tacky's enthusiasm. "Well, if you think you can get rid of him, good luck to you. As far as I'm concerned, one fox more or less is neither here nor there. There are plenty around the coombe, you can be sure."

"Ah, but there's none like this one, Mr Granger. This one is something special," Tacky beamed as he pulled on his hat and untied Tiger's piece of string from the leg of the chair. "I'll be on my way an' see what I can do. Don't 'ee worry, Mr Granger, us'll get 'un. Crafty though 'ee may be, us'll get 'un."

Tacky trudged from Ravenscoombe with a new sense of purpose. He reached the Ashton road and turned downhill to walk the mile and a half to the King's Head. He would have to tell the lunchtime regulars about the grey fox.

CHAPTER 5

DEEP IN THE badger sett, the grey fox slept away the accumulated fatigue of the previous twenty-four hours. Vaguely into his mind came the sound of the yapping terrier, but it was mixed with images of the pack. Convulsed with his dream, the fox woke for a fleeting second, then tucked his nose further under his brush and went back to sleep. The air seeping down from the wood above began to chill as daylight waned, and he shivered, turned and settled again, but the deepening cold aggravated his hunger and drove his consciousness to the surface so that reluctantly he uncurled, stretched and began to scramble up towards the dimming circle of light that marked the entrance.

Normally he would have paused just inside, scented the air and then whipped out and away quickly and smoothly before any prying eyes could see his going. But this time he stopped and sniffed for several seconds, because something had changed. There was a new scent that had not been there before and the long grey hairs at the nape of his neck began to prickle. He recognised the smell of carrion flesh and it brought the saliva to his mouth.

For a brief moment he was tempted to rush out and take the meat, but the warning sensation was still there at the base of his skull to countermand his desire, and it made him pause just long enough to intensify his suspicion. He turned and squeezed along a side tunnel to find the opening blocked, where a strong man scent made him forget his hunger. He backed out and tried the other bolt hole, but again was met by a man-tainted barrier. Once more, he sought the entrance as panic welled up to blur his thoughts. He had braced himself to bolt through the opening when suddenly there was a flurry of brown feathers outside. The swish of pinions on snow startled the fox into immobility and he crouched motionless as the buzzard sank her strong talons into the meat and thrashed the air until she wrenched it free. He waited while she flapped lazily up to her fork in the elm, then he flopped on to his belly while his brain assimilated the messages his nose and eyes had brought.

The critical moment of panic was past and the tension in the taut body relaxed. He knew he was in danger, but now his brain was working again. Slowly, he pushed his nose out until it touched cold wire, and he instantly recoiled, sensing the strangeness of things there that had not been there before. The metal smell was all around the entrance. It was unknown, and therefore dangerous. Other ways out were blocked and man-scented, so he would have to make a new way.

He began to scratch the soil away from the side of the hole, gradually enlarging the entrance. He tore his pads on sharp stones and gnawed through tree roots, digging furiously until the gap was large enough for him to squeeze through. The wire tilted as he brushed past, leaving the snare unsprung.

The still air held the fox's breath as he padded down the track from the old quarry. His recent danger, only partly realised, was quickly forgotten in the need to satisfy his appetite. Suddenly he changed course, scrambled up the side of the cleeve and set off for Trenden Wood at a fast lope.

In the open country, an even whiteness kept night at bay long enough to give wood pigeons badly-needed time to forage the sheltered spots on unploughed headlands where the young barley, self-sown from last year's harvest, was already struggling to life beneath the snow. The evening sky faded, apple green to indigo, as reluctantly, one by one, they took off to glide into the evergreens, slapping their wings in warning as the fox slid beneath them. He was following the exact route by which he had fled from the wood twenty-four hours earlier. As soon as the blackness of the spruce plantation enveloped him, he stopped poised, perfectly still, until the countless tiny rustlings ceased, and the inhabitants accepted his presence. Only then did his legs slowly fold under him until he rested on his belly, ears cocked and eyes alert.

A single dead leaf on a stunted oak sapling began to fidget as the night breeze sifted through the trees, and the fox's sharp ears caught the faint flick as its withered surface twisted. He moved slightly to face it so that his sensitive nose could pick up the messages brought on the wind, then he settled down again with his snout resting between outstretched forepaws. Above his head, the herringbone pattern of branches and sky faded to charcoal and became a single darkness, matching the dimness of the forest floor. Scattered patches of snow slowly stiffened with a thin crust of rime, but still the fox remained motionless.

A slight noise brought his head up, but it was only snow dislodged by roosting blackbird as she ruffed her feathers against the cold. He listened hard for a few moments and then resumed his wait. Again, his head went up and this time a double pat-pat was followed quickly by another and another. He turned his head towards the sound, monitoring its progress with ears and nose, and at the same time he gradually stood up. It was as if his legs had simply grown downwards to lift his body, so smooth and natural was the movement. He stretched forward, stiff-legged, and began to move, placing each hind foot exactly where the corresponding forefoot had rested. The pat-pat was closer and he waited, belly close to the ground and one foot raised, while the rabbit searched the snow-free carpet for shoots of brome grass. The fox could see nothing, but his nose pin-pointed the quarry with deadly accuracy and he selected a spot which would bring it within easy reach. The rabbit fed nervously, and abruptly changed direction. The fox countered and, moving only when the rabbit did, selected another position. Again, the rabbit turned, and the fox moved with it, this time more rapidly, closing the gap until he was once more within springing distance, then, feeling for a secure hold with his hind feet, he drew them under his body, rocked twice, and leapt. His front pads hit the rabbit squarely in mid-back and at the same time the long canines met through its spine. It knew and felt nothing.

He ate the rabbit on the spot, leaving only a few pinches of grey and buff fur to drift over the snow. For a few moments, he sat taking in the night sounds, his long tongue licking the last fragments from his jowl, then he yawned with a guttural "Yaark!", listened and suddenly leapt into the air and began to run.

He ran for the joy of running, his whole body responding to a deep urge to quit the wood. Using his tail as a rudder, he scurried between the close trunks, skittering and throwing up showers of dead needles. He reached the ride where the snow was deeper and plunged head first to roll in its smooth whiteness, then over the ride and into the hard woods, past gnarled columns of oak and the smooth grey trunks of ash and sycamore. He followed the downhill gradient at an effortless lope until, with a last flounder through a snow-filled ditch, he found himself in a flat open field.

For a moment, he paused to listen, then with a quick shake, he was off again across the field, tongue lolling and ears flattened. He stopped on the far side where a laid hedge barred the way, then he trotted down the head land looking for a gap. Suddenly, his ears pricked. It was no more than a faint sound on the wind, but the reply welled up inside and he threw back his head and called his hoarse "Yaark!". Twice he repeated it and then launched himself at the thorn hedge to scramble out on the other side, scratched and bleeding. Now he knew where he was going, but as yet had no notion why.

He gave no heed to find cover, but travelled in a straight line across open fields and cottage gardens as though drawn by an invisible and unbreakable thread. Every few minutes, he stopped and stood poised until the thread tugged again and he was off once more, past the straggling buildings of Menaridden where Tarquin's howl set the pack singing. Through the sheep field and the last of the kale, the fox went on to the flat expanse of meadowland and into the small copse beyond.

The vixen sat by the fallen remains of a stricken elm, and when she scented the young fox, she screamed again, and the sound echoed from the trees and out across the frozen landscape, drawing a response from the dog fox so that he knew why he had come. They met in a clearing where woodmen had burned the small elm branches and left piles of cord wood for the Menaridden fires. Stiff-legged, they approached each other, both cautious, both looking for the sign that would break the barriers. It came from the vixen, who suddenly rolled over and exposed the cream fur of her throat. The grey fox stood over her for a moment, his fangs bared, then backed away as the vixen squirmed up to him, mouth open. The scent of the female soothed and excited him, imprinting a new and strange pattern of behaviour so that he pranced and bounded with tail held high round and round the vixen, each circle bringing him nearer until she ended his cavorting by giving him a hard nip behind the shoulder, then both animals dashed out of the clearing, through the copse and into the meadow.

They ran side by side, but always the vixen chose the paths, leading them deeper into her own territory of big fields and slow-running rivers that formed the rich farmlands of Ashton Vale. She ran quickly, but the grey fox was of a long-legged moorland breed and kept up with an easy tireless stride. He had long lost all sense of direction, for now his whole being was consumed by the chemistry of reproducing his kind.

So oblivious was he that he neither heard nor scented the twenty-five pounds of raw fury that hurtled at him from the corner of a forestry plantation. The grey fox was knocked sideways as the older and heavier suitor hit him full in the ribs. The first the young fox knew about it was the pain of long canines raking the loose skin of his neck, then the weight of impact pushing the breath from his body.

Pain dispelled the euphoria and the grey fox came to his feet bristling with rage. His opponent was a big, sandy dog fox that lorded the plantations of spruce and fir where the River Asher broadened out to form the estuary. He too had heard the vixen's call and had crossed the river by the main road bridge in the face of a dozen headlamps. Now the two rivals snarled at each other, their amber eyes narrowed with hatred. The grey fox was the first to lunge and he took a mouthful of sandy fur from the plantation fox's shoulder. The latter turned quickly and both animals reared on their hind legs to push jowl to jowl until they rolled over, squealing and biting in a flurry of grey and yellow, while the vixen watched impassively from a nearby gorse clump.

The snow, alternatively churned and flattened, turned to half-frozen slush, making it difficult for the contestants to keep their feet. Gradually, the bigger fox worked himself uphill until he had the advantage of the slope. The grey fox was quicker, but he had travelled a greater distance and was tiring rapidly. The stand-up fight became a running battle with the grey fox slithering downhill towards the deceptively smooth surface of a snow-filled ditch. He turned to parry his opponent's lunge, lost his footing and tumbled tail first into the drift, to land on his back in the half-liquid mud at the bottom. He was up in a second, took one look at the big dog fox towering over him from the field above and ran.

Twice he circled the field until his direction was sure, then he set his mark towards the high country and Ravenscoombe.

CHAPTER 6

THE BACK DOOR slammed shut and Clegg stood for a moment to accustom his eyes to the gloom. He reached for the tilly lamp that hung from a bracket next to the door, primed and lit it with methodical precision, noting that the mantle was torn and would soon need replacing. He pumped until the lamp burned bright, then hung it from an iron hook in the ceiling cross-beam. "Ah, that's better," he said to the collie as Skipper pushed past him to sniff round the kitchen table for any missed scraps before padding over to his basket to flop down on the mud-spattered, dog-haired piece of blanket that made the place home to him.

It had been a hard day working the sheep in deep snow, and there had been hay bales to carry and water to fetch in buckets from the stream, for all the outside taps were frozen solid. Clegg was tired and stiff, and wearily removed his waterproofs and wellingtons, then with a grunt, he sat down on one of the three kitchen chairs, not daring to settle in his armchair lest he fall asleep before the evening chores were done.

He listened to Skipper's snuffling as the dog cleaned himself and hunted for fleas. The clock in the corner ticked with a strangely deadened sound, the snow outside seeming to muffle all noise so that even the familiar rustling and chomping of animals in the yard was cut off and silenced. Clegg's left hand absently rubbed an aching knee as in his mind he went through the process of making up the fire and preparing a meal, as though thinking about it would get the work done. The damp chill of the room seeped through his sweater and he willed his aching muscles to move until a shiver convulsed his shoulders and he stood up, kicking the chair away as he moved to thrust a log into the greying embers of the fire. A small patch of red glowed and broke into flame. The dry wood crackled and he stood over it, guarding the tender flicker until it strengthened and grew, while he soaked up the warmth and gazed hypnotically at the changing patterns until the clock chimed seven.

"Better get some supper on the go," he said out loud to himself, switching on the small transistor radio which stood on the window ledge above the kitchen sink. A disc jockey's cheery banter brought in the outside world for a few moments ... "And now, from The 5th Dimension ... " There followed a loud cacophony of noise, of electric guitars and voices hoarse and raucous, yet strangely alive and compelling. He listened for a few seconds and thought of Stephen. "Honestly, Dad, I can do my homework better with it on ... "

Clegg signed and, with a quick movement, switched it off before his mind dwelt too long on the past with its memories and recriminations. "Never feel sorry for yourself," he spoke out loud again, pondering the grease and egg stains of the day's washing-up which lay higgledy-piggledy in the chipped enamel bowl. Skipper raised one ear and continued snuffling.

Clegg decided to put off the washing-up until after supper and took a clean plate and utensils from the sideboard, then he set about the meal.

"Something to think about, something to do, that's the answer, eh, Skipper?" The smell of fried sausages filled the room, and Skipper salivated and resurrected a bleached bone from the depths of the blanket to gnaw until his time for supper came.

When they had eaten, and the last plate had been washed and put away, Clegg threw another log on the fire and settled into his armchair. After a few minutes, he turned off the lamp and sat by the firelight. The embers glowed and flickered, and his thoughts drifted back to childhood when he sat by the great open fire in his grandparent's farmhouse ... Christmas and the whole family roasting chestnuts, the grown-ups talking family gossip and the children playing with their new toys, while the old couple sat back to bask in the warmth of the fire and the occasion. Then, before the younger ones went to bed, they would turn out the lights and search for shapes in the fire.

"Look, there's an elephant."

"Where?"

"There, look. That bit of wood is its trunk."

"That's not an elephant. It's more like a tank."

He had dreamed of it being like that at Ravenscoombe with Cathy and Stephen. Perhaps he should have bought that diesel generator and got electric light into the place, but it had seemed more important to buy those extra draft ewes at the time. Anyway, this was a farm, not a luxury hotel. "First things first," he had told his wife. "It's the sheep and cattle that earn our bread and butter, not electric gadgets in every room."

But he had intended to get the generator as soon as the flock began to show a reasonable profit. He half-turned to the dog in the corner. "The trouble with women is they can't wait," he said louder than necessary so that Skipper jumped suddenly and hung his head as he recognised the edge in the voice. "Can't wait," he repeated. "Want everything at once." Clegg subsided into his chair once more and fell silent.

The clock rumbled and ground out nine tinny chimes. Clegg started and looked at his wristwatch. "Fast again," he mumbled and leant forward to aim a vicious lunge at the half-burned log with the piece of angle iron that served as a poker. The shower of sparks lit the room for a brief moment, and in the dimness of his corner, Skipper yawned and stretched until he overlapped the basket at both ends.

Clegg got up and put the hands of the clock back a quarter of an hour. He sat down again, only to get up almost immediately and light the lamp. He looked towards the dog basket.

"At ten o'clock, we'll do the rounds of the ewes." The dog's snores continued unabated. "Skipper! God, dog! Come here!" A snort, the rattle of claws on lino and the dog pushed his nose beneath Clegg's outstretched hand. "I said, we'll go and look at the ewes at ten o'clock. Can't afford to let that damned fox get any more, can we?" The black and white tail moved imperceptibly as the collie stretched at full-length to expose his belly to the fire. "You couldn't care less really," Clegg sighed and reached down to scratch the dog's ribs. "Tell you what. We'll do the rounds at half past nine tonight."

Skipper returned to his basket, and his dream, and eventually Clegg, too, dozed in his chair.

He awoke with a start and glanced up at the clock. He had been asleep for over an hour. He poked the log to send a shower of sparks up the chimney, then, reluctant to move, settled back again to wait for the flame to die. It was nearly midnight by the time he roused himself and went out to do his rounds.

The night was cold and clear, and the fresh snow crunched underfoot. Clegg suddenly remembered the hound. He had meant to feed him after supper. "Poor brute," he said to himself. "He must be famished by now." He went back and made a warm mash of bran and milk, mixing in what few scraps of meat he could find, then, with a jug of water to replenish the water bowl, he made his way to the loft.

Warrior got up and stretched as he went in. A good sign, Clegg thought, as it showed that the pain had lessened. The old hound even raised a growl for Skipper as Clegg put the dish of food in front of him. "Well, you seem to be on the mend, old chap. No doubt Squire What's-his-name will be up for you in the morning and you'll both be out chasing round the countryside again before the week's out." He watched the hound gulp the mash before putting some fresh dry straw down where snow had filtered through.

Satisfied that the animal would be comfortable, he went outside, bolting the door behind him.

Behind the loft, the ground rose steeply through an old orchard where the distorted trunks of neglected trees stood like rows of drunken revellers, frozen into black statues, their gnarled and twisted figures holding the

Plough's seven stars. It was as Clegg turned to descend the steps that he saw a movement - a shadow flick across a line of trees. He switched off his torch and waited, catching hold of Skipper's nape and hissing him quiet. The shadow crossed the white snow and paused, to become a stump among other stumps. It moved again, and Clegg knew it was the fox. He could hold the collie no longer. It tore free and, with an excited yelp, bounded over the low stone wall into the orchard.

The grey fox was startled by the noise. He was confused and tired after his long run from the meadowland. He plunged down the slope as the collie rushed towards him and they met in a flurry of snow. But, tired though he was, the fox's reactions were fractions of a second faster than the dog's and he was able to swerve past towards the buildings. Skipper snorted and turned as the snow hit his muzzle. He paused for a second and then followed the fox helter-skelter down the hill to where the white roof of the loft jutted out from the hillside. In a desperate effort to avoid the collie's teeth, the fox leapt at the sloping roof and began to scramble towards the ridge. The hound below gave tongue, and a slate moved and showered him with fox-tainted snow, then another slate fell and another. The fox's pads clawed at rotten laths and he found himself falling into the blackness of the loft.

He fell among the hay bales, but was on his feet immediately, twisting to face the frantic hound six feet below him. Warrior jumped at the bales and the untidy stack crumbled. Fox and hound fell together, biting and snarling. The old hound was stiff, and his ribs still pained him. He was no match for the young fox which moved like quicksilver between his legs to take hold of one ear with needle-sharp teeth. The dog shook his head violently, spinning the fox across the loft as Clegg opened the door to sort out the rumpus. The fox hesitated for a second, then made a desperate lunge at the dog's jowl and, while the old hound was still shaking his head, slipped past Clegg and out into the night.

Clegg closed the door quickly before Warrior could follow, for he had no desire to lose the hound, which he surely would if it picked up the trail of the departed fox. The old dog howled his fury and pain so that Clegg returned to the kitchen for more bread and milk and antiseptic for the wounds, while Warrior licked his own blood and tasted the scent of the grey fox.

After all the excitement, Clegg had to shut Skipper in the coal shed, for the dog was nearly demented. He trudged round his alerted flock, each ewe looking nervously towards the buildings and the source of the noise. Clegg spoke to them reassuringly and they turned to watch him, hoping for food. He searched the hedge bank for separated ewes that might be ready to lamb and was relieved to find none. Satisfied he could leave them until morning, he took a last look at the Blackface ewe and her twins and returned to the house.

The clock struck one as Clegg made himself a cup of tea to take with him to his cold bedroom,

CHAPTER 7

TACKY BOWDEN was up next morning well before dawn, and with shotgun and flashlight, he picked his way over the fields into Colspit Wood, his terrier at his heels. Was it old age or excitement that quickened his heartbeat as he approached the sett? He stopped for a moment to get his breath and push a cartridge into the breach of the gun, then calling Tiger to heel, he began the climb to where he had set the snare.

The torch picked out a dark shape beside the opening. Tacky gasped "We've got 'un!" He pushed off the safety catch. The dark shape was motionless. He fired one shot at it and saw the soil spurt up, then knew as he lowered the gun that it was not the fox. As he scrambled up, he saw that the dark shape was the enlarged opening. He picked up the snare and pushed it into his overcoat pocket and while Tiger lingered round the hole, he made his way back, muttering to himself. "This 'un's a real crafty begger. Us'll 'ave to think again if we to catch that ol' grey devil, blowed if us won't."

The old man paused as he reached the Ashton road. It was full light and the wind lifted the powdered snow in tiny whirlwinds and laid the tarmac bare. He screwed up his face and blinked the water from his eyes. "Wind's changed," he informed the terrier. "'Tis goin' to be a sharp 'un, no mistake.'" He shook his head, pulled at his collar and trudged on towards his cottage. The cold north-easterly wind swept the sky, leaving high cirrus and mares' tails on a sharp blue horizon. By the time he reached home, the mixture of snow and black mud in Tacky's gateway had hardened into piebald rock which he kicked tentatively, sucking the air through his teeth and shaking his head as a sign of foreboding and disapproval. "'Tis goin' to be a sharp 'un," he repeated.

He fried his breakfast and mulled over the events of the past twenty-four hours. Since the death of his wife and giving up the farm, his life had settled into an almost changeless pattern of caring for his few livestock, a daily walk of half a mile to the King's Head and a weekly trip the extra half-mile to the village shops and the Post Office for his pension. Every Christmas, he received a card from his only daughter in New Zealand. His few lifelong friends were, as Tacky would put it, "Gone afore," and he knew that to the customers of the saloon bar in the King's Head, he was no longer "Farmer" Bowden, but just old Tacky. The events concerning the grey fox had given him something new to think about and a good excuse to visit his old home in Ravenscoombe. It was this that gave him most satisfaction that morning: to see the old place again and walk the familiar fields and woods. It had not saddened him to enter the house and see the belongings of another occupant as it would have done his Edith, for home to Tacky was the farm and the fields and the dark tangle of Colspit Wood, and they did not change.

And so, as he sat down to eat his breakfast, his thoughts turned to Ravenscoombe and its present owner. He cut off the bacon rind and gave it to Tiger. "Four generations o' we Bowdens farmed the coombe," he confided to the dog. "Four generations," he repeated, wiping the plate with his bread. "Poor ol' father would turn in 'is grave if 'ee knew we were out of the place."

He drew the back of his hand across his mouth, then poured himself a mug of dark brown tea and sat back to contemplate the large sepia photograph of Bowden senior which covered up a damp patch next to the over large dresser. A square face was made even squarer by the grey beard that fringed the jaw while the clean-shaven upper lip revealed a thin, hard mouth. It was the face of a man who had struggled with the poor soil, the rocks and the steep gradients of Ravenscoombe, a man who had fought the wind and incessant rain and had held his own. He had been a man inordinately proud of his family's long history at Ravenscoombe, and Tacky could hear his words now: "Roots, boy, roots, that's what's important. A man should be able to die in the house he was born in."

Tacky looked at the photograph. "Ah, well, no good you lecturin' me now. 'Tis all over an' done with. I were always too easy goin', that's the trouble. Not like you, you ol' bugger." He sighed and moved over to the sink. "An' what do 'ee think o' the new chap then, eh?" he asked, looking down at the terrier. "Not a bad sort, a bit quiet mind, but on the 'ole, not a bad sort."

Tacky nodded and began washing up. "Mind 'ee, t'is a pity about 'is missus a-runnin' off like that, but 'ee never can tell wi' women. No matter what a man does, t'is never enough." He glanced at the picture of his wife on the dresser, and paused for a moment, cup in hand, before continuing with a shrug, "'Ee works 'ard, I'll say that for 'un. Does is best to keep the farm right, 'im being from the town an' all, so I reckon it could be worse."

The washing-up finished, Tacky tidied the room and sat down again to think. "Now, about this ol' grey fox. 'Tidn' right that such a 'ard-working chap should be plagued by the likes of 'ee. 'Twould never 'ave happened in Father's day. E'd 'uv 'ad 'un, sure as eggs. Ah, an' us'll get un' too." He fondled the dog's ears, "Mr Granger don't know about such things so us'll 'ave to give 'un a hand."

There and then, he decided that as soon as he had tended his livestock, he would walk to Ravenscoombe to look for the fox's tracks. Foxes, he knew, were creatures of habit, so if he could locate the runs in the snow, he stood a better chance of trapping his victim when the thaw came, if not before.

He went out to feed his pigs which were kept in a variety of huts, old railway box vans and a wheelless cattle wagon, all of which were surrounded by a sea of frozen mud. The six black and white Saddleback sows and their various offspring were fed on a slop of barley meal, fishmeal and water which Tacky ladled into granite troughs dotted about the little paddock. He had to spend half an hour thawing the outside water pipe while the ribby matrons squealed and rooted the black frozen clods in their eagerness.

The chickens took less time and had a scattering of small corn (the 'seconds' of wheat unsuitable for milling which he bought straight off the combine as cheaply as possible in September). He collected one egg and came out of the van muttering that his poor fowls had been put off lay "by that damned grey fox".

These jobs completed, Tacky returned to the kitchen to equip himself for the reconnaissance. He put on an extra pair of socks, khaki woollen mittens and a blue balaclava helmet, on top of which he crammed his trilby hat. From a stand near the back door, he selected a blackthorn stick, slung his poaching bag and a battered pair of binoculars over his shoulder and, with Tiger at his heels, set out for Colspit Wood.

An orange-yellow sun tipped the ridge above the Ashton road as man and dog laboured down the slope of the first field. Tacky recalled the unending fight against the bracken that infested the pockets of deeper soil. He had always considered the field well named - Higher Brownhill - for brown it was from September to July until new fronds once again hid last year's decay. Now all was smooth whiteness, for winter had drawn a veil over the land's blemishes, and rocks and gorse had become merely hummocks in a white landscape, broken only by the zigzag pattern of tracks left by the man and the dog.

Tiger excitedly followed a line of prints that came out of a gorse clump by the field wall. Pairs of oval indents two inches long with a single round dot between each pair, they disappeared through a gap between the stones, leaving a yellow stain and a few small round droppings. Tacky called the dog, muttered, "Rabbit, a young 'un," and walked on.

Over the wall in Lower Brownhill, another set of tracks held his attention more closely. A double line of round prints, neat and clear, came down from the Ashton road in a straight line and carried on in the direction of Ravenscoombe Farm. After a few seconds, however, he pronounced "Cat!" and struck off at right angles towards Colspit.

In the wood, he noticed where blackbirds had cleared the snow under the holly trees, scattering the dark leaf mould in their search for the dormant insects and half-rotten holly berries. Further down, a line of large bird prints ended in a fan of wing marks, and a single curled feather, the colour of burnished copper, showed that a cock pheasant had taken flight. Tacky kept his eyes to the ground, particularly as he neared the old badger sett. He paused over a single indent in the snow and picked up a soft buff feather which lay beside two tiny pinpricks of red, the spot where a wood owl had struck a short-tailed vole as it travelled its runs beneath the snow. He examined the sett carefully to make sure the fox was not there before following the cart track into the old quarry and up the narrow path into the field above.

It was a warm climb and by the time he had reached the stone wall at the top, he had taken off the balaclava helmet and mittens and was mopping his bald head with a red-spotted handkerchief. He propped his backside against the wall and, unslinging the glasses, he scanned the whole coombe from Colspit Wood, sweeping up to the High Moor, and beyond to Cragg Tor. An uneven patch of white in the corner of the next field was the focal point of his attention. He knew it consisted of a brake of gorse and brambles that covered a stony outcrop, and with plenty of crevices and cover, it was just the place for a fox to kennel in cold weather. Tacky guessed it was riddled with rabbit runs and he could see quite plainly the criss-cross of rabbit tracks that patterned the snow on the eastern edge where the sun's early rays had softened the crust. But there was one set of marks unlike the others: a single line, straight and deep which went into the brake and did not emerge. Tacky grunted, rammed the glasses into their case and set off to investigate.

Long before he got there, he was sure he was on the track of the grey fox.

Nevertheless, he examined the pad marks carefully, noting the single straight line and the presence of hair between the toe prints, indicating that no dog had made them. They were not quite as round as those tracks he had identified as belonging to a cat, and as he traced the line back to where the snow was deeper, he saw the unmistakable indent of a broad tail. The old man gave a satisfied "Ah!", straightened his back and stood for a moment, rubbing his aching hip with the palm of his hand. "Fox!" he said, nodding his head slowly." 'Tis that damned grey for sure."

The fact that it could have been any other fox did not cross Tacky's mind. This had to be the grey fox, he was sure of it. He felt it in his bones. He walked around the brake, looking for enlarged runs through the brambles that could be used by a fox, all the while keeping Tiger close on his string, for he did not want the fox bolted until he had set some wires. Wherever he found a well-trodden run, he pegged a snare, seven in all. "If at first you don't succeed ... " he chanted, keeping time as he banged in the last peg with a stone, " ... try, try, try again. There!" With a final whack, he flung the stone over the wall and stood up, well satisfied with his work. "Now us'll just 'ave to wait an' see," he said quietly to the dog as he slung his bag over his shoulder and began the descent towards the stream. At the bottom, he bathed his face in the icy water before crossing the clapper bridge and starting up the other side of the valley towards the Ashton road.

Tacky reached the road just as Josh Huccaby's Land Rover turned down track towards Ravenscoombe Farm. The vehicle slid to a halt and Josh leaned out.

"Morning, Thomas!" he called as the old man stood in the gateway waiting for the Land Rover to pass, half hoping he had not been seen. It gave Tacky a strange feeling to be called by his proper name for once. In fact, Josh Huccaby was the only person locally who still used it, and there were many in the village who had no idea that Tacky was not the name bestowed at christening. Only the few contemporaries still in Ashton remembered Thomas Ackland Bowden, named after his great-grandfather who built the mill at Ravenscoombe and owned most of the land between Ashton and the Menaridden Valley where the Hubbacys, Josh's great-grandfather, scratched a living milking the cows which were kept on the waterlogged meadows. It had taken a very short time for the village school to shorten Thomas Ackland to 'Tacky' and the name had stuck.

Tacky looked and felt uncomfortable as he shuffled over. "Mornin', Josh." There was an awkward silence while Josh began to feel embarrassed, conscious of the old man's change in circumstances, painfully revealed by his tattered coat and the hat with the dark sweat patches above the hat band.

Josh strove for something to say. "Haven't seen you for a long time, not since ... " He was about to say, "not since that blazing hot county show when the pigs died of heat stroke," when he remembered that it was at that show that Edith Bowden had collapsed while Tacky was being entertained by the feed merchant to whom he owed most money. By the time they had found him, she was dead and he was too drunk to realise it. Josh coughed and repeated, "Haven't seen you for a long time."

Tacky nodded. "Ah, that's true, that's very true, but you'll the same as ever, Josh. Why, it don't seem more'n yesterday that you used to ride your little ol' pony over to 'elp Father and me break they colts."

Josh smiled. He remembered well cantering Twinkle across the moor from Menaridden and down into the next valley to visit the Bowdens. Old man Bowden had bred some useful ponies in his time, but his gift for horseflesh had not been passed on to his son. Thomas Ackland was too ham-fisted and short-tempered to break ponies, and in any case, by the time young Josh had come on the scene, Tacky was well into his twenties and far too heavy for the little animals. Still, it had riled Tacky to hear his father say that the ten-year-old Josh "had the gift" and that he had not.

And so they spoke of old times, and neither asked the other's business in Ravenscoombe, nor did they dwell on matters that might have been hurtful to either of them, then having passed the time of day they parted, and Josh let in the clutch and drove on. The steering wheel bucked as the front wheels hit the frozen ruts beneath the snow. He pushed the lever into four-wheel drive, grinding round the bends in bottom gear while the vehicle slithered and shook at each dip in the track.

As he pulled into the yard, Warrior, recognising the distinctive sound of the none too healthy diesel engine, set up a howl that caused a beaming Josh to call out in his high pitched huntsman's voice, "Whoop, my boy! Good dog, Warrior! There's a good feller!" The old hound bayed in ecstasy at the cracked, discordant sounds which drew all the love and affection he had to give.

Clegg was already in the yard and leading the way to the loft. Josh caught him up, panting up the steep steps, saying excitedly, "The old hound's in fine song then? Can't have come to much harm, that's a relief." Then, remembering himself, he continued in a more subdued tone of voice, "Er, sorry I couldn't get over to fetch him yesterday, but we couldn't get out until the snow plough had cleared the Ashton road."

Clegg nodded and pushed open the door. A tan avalanche descended on the man following him and Josh all but fell down the steps as the old hound thumped two great paws on to his chest to slaver over the beloved face.

"Get down, you daft ha'path! All right, that's enough!" Half-annoyed, half-laughing, Josh grabbed Warrior by the scruff of his neck and pushed him down the steps in front of him. "I see he's torn an ear and got a nick on the jowl. Didn't notice those the other night."

He looked up inquiringly, then Clegg began to explain about the grey fox falling through the roof and wondered if it sounded at all credible. He decided it didn't and invited Josh to have a look for himself. So they bundled Warrior into the back of the Land Rover and went back up to the loft. Josh looked at the hole in the roof and picked up some grey hairs from a fallen lath. He inspected the tumbled bales and sniffed noisily before turning to Clegg with a grin. "Well, there's no doubt about it, you've had a fox through your roof, and that's one for the book." His face clouded. "But look here, I seem to have caused you a deal of trouble. Let me send a chap over to put that hole right."

Clegg frowned and shook his head. "No, thank you," he said. "In any case, it was my dog that caused the commotion, not yours."

Josh did not press the point. "Well, I'm most grateful, Mr Granger, and I'm sorry for any inconvenience we've caused."

They shook hands and Clegg shrugged. "Oh, it's not your fault," he said, "it's that damned fox. You'd never credit so much damage could be done by one animal. First it takes one of my lambs right out of the buildings here, then it has five of Mr Bowden's hens, and finishes up by falling through my roof and biting your foxhound, and all in two days."

Josh smiled. "He's quite a character is this grey fox of ours. I thought old Bowden looked a bit put out when I saw him just now. Well, we'll have to watch out for this one. If he's been into the buildings once, he'll be certain to come again, particularly if we get some hard weather." He paused for a moment, then continued, "Look, the hunt is due to meet at the King's Head in a couple of weeks' time. If you're agreeable, Mr Granger, I'd like to draw through your farm and we'll see if we can get him." He turned towards the Land Rover, then as an afterthought turned back to look Clegg full in the face. "If we've got to kill him, let's do it right, Mr Granger. I want no wounded foxes taking three weeks to die of lead poisoning, nor any of old Bowden's traps and snares. I've seen too many three-legged foxes for that. If my hounds catch him, he'll be dead and right quick. If they don't, he'll be away free and in one piece, none the worse for his experience, and that's how it should be, Mr Granger. I hope you agree." He spoke the last words emphatically, as one used to being taken notice of.

Clegg's frown deepened. He wanted to be rid of the pestering fox but objected strongly to the 'squire of the manor' tone adopted by the older man. It reminded him of all that he detested in the life he had given up, where money was authority and authority was power. "I do not enjoy killing animals in any way at all, Mr Huccaby; in fact, I would greatly prefer it if you would simply chase the creature out of my valley so that it didn't come back."

It was Josh's turn to shrug. "I'm sorry," he said quietly. "I didn't mean to get on my high horse. Believe it or not, I do not enjoy the killing part myself, neither does anyone else that I know of, but it has to be done one way or another and I just happen to think that my way is best."

Clegg watched the Land Rover climb the track with the tan head of old Warrior sticking out from under the canopy, and it struck him that every one was making a great deal of fuss about one fox. "They've probably got nothing better to do," he muttered as he walked back to the lambing field to finish building the half-dozen lambing pens of straw bales and corrugated iron, for the flock was starting to lamb in earnest.

CHAPTER 8

CLEGG FINISHED the last pen as the sky became just dark enough to show the first star. He weighted the final sheet of tin down with large stones from the hedge bottom, blew the warmth into his frozen fingers, and with his tool bag slung over his shoulders, he made his way to the farm buildings to start the evening chores.

The first star was joined by another, and a heron flapped lazily from Stannon Marsh, trailing his long legs across a deepening sky on his way to the unfrozen mud flats of the estuary. The frost bit into the land and men barred their doors against it and prepared themselves for the long darkness.

At Menaridden, Isobel Huccaby turned up the central heating and switched on her electric blanket, while Tacky Bowden stacked his fireplace with split oak logs and laid an old horse rug over the foot of his bed.

The night settled into a cold stillness which reached into the bramble thicket and touched the grey fox so that he started up and listened intently. But he heard nothing, for all creatures had fallen silent in order to conserve the energy they would need to face the oncoming cold. His brain was still alive with the sensations evoked by his meeting with the vixen, and he had an overriding impulse to leave the valley for the open moorland to seek a mate among the rocks and heather beyond Cragg Tor.

He scrambled out of the shallow depression between two rocks, which had sheltered him from the daylight cold. Now he was stiff and hungry and, anxious to get his limbs going, he ran along the largest rabbit run towards the arch of briars that led to the open. His nose sensed the cold air and at the same time the warning metal smell he had experienced at the badger sett, but he was moving too quickly and as his forepaws grooved the snow in a desperate effort to stop, the wire noose tightened with a jerk around his neck.

For several seconds, the grey fox lay stunned, then he moved, and the wire pulled tighter so that his breath came in hoarse gasps. Now fear and panic blanketed his mind so that he shook and struggled against the thing that held him, while all the time it gripped him more firmly, until at last, exhausted and near unconsciousness, he lay still in the snow.

The barn owl, ghosting the hedge banks, swooped low over him, brushing the tallest bramble with soft wings. The tiny scattering of snow it caused showered down through the dead purple leaves to powder the fox's body, but he did not move. Within the thicket, the rabbits lost their fear and began to search for food. Dimly in his mind, the fox heard the patter, patter, but now he had no hunger, only pain and with it a calmness, the calmness that comes before death.

In the long hours before dawn, the grey fox stirred. Far away, beyond Cragg Tor, a vixen had screamed, and the sound rekindled the spark of consciousness in the stricken fox's brain. He opened his eyes and saw the glint of wire in the starlight. He tried to bite through it, and although the action was futile, it caused him to move and the movement pushed back death. The vixen screamed again and suddenly the grey fox lurched to his feet in a last desperate effort to rid himself of the pain that gripped his neck. The upward jerk loosened the iron peg that held the snare and as the fox flung himself towards the far-off sound, the peg pulled out sideways and he rolled down the slope with the wire and peg trailing behind him.

The tightness around his neck had eased enough for him to breathe properly. Gingerly, he tried moving, and although the wire pulled taut with the weight of the iron peg, it no longer throttled him when he tugged at it. He attempted to scratch off the pain, first with one hind leg and then the other, managing to pull open the noose until one ear slipped through, but it pulled tight again round his neck as soon as he moved. Eventually, he turned towards Colspit Wood and, dragging the iron peg behind him, crawled into the shelter of the old mill ruin to find seclusion beneath an overhang of ivy in one corner. As dawn outlined the roofless gabled wall, the fox gnawed at the metal that tormented him, but the wire was new and firmly attached to the peg. It grated his teeth and out into his gums but would not part.

The barn owl glided through the gaping hole that was once a window and swept up to his niche above the fox where it wheezed and snuffled and finally slept. The grey fox also slept, but his was the sleep of exhaustion and shock, full of pain and fitful wakings until eventually he too was eased into oblivion as a fresh fall of snow sifted through the ivy.

When the snow cleared, the land was wiped clean. The sun rose to its zenith in a clear sky and every icicle on the corrugated iron sheets of the lambing pens held a glistening droplet. The ewes quietly chewed their cud while the lambs lay close against them for warmth. Clegg carried out more hay and scattered it in long lines across the paddock, at the same time studying the flock, noting the ewes that looked close to lambing. According to his diary, at least a dozen would lamb within the next few days, for he had marked the ram's chest with coloured dye the previous autumn so that the raddle indicated which ewes had been served and when. Now the hundred and forty-seven days of pregnancy were up for the first batch and from now on Clegg would have to keep a constant vigil to ensure the minimum losses in ewes and lambs.

As the shadows lengthened, a ewe detached herself from the flock and sought a sheltered spot in the far corner of the field, first scraping the snow with one forefoot before settling down with her back to the flock to chew the cud between the slight spasms of pain.

Thick grey cloud once more filled the sky, the droplets froze to the tips of the icicles and the slush in front of the pens hardened to ice. The snow came in large heavy flakes, covering the solitary sheep so that she remained unnoticed when the rest of the flock were gathered for the night. She moved closer to the hedge to find shelter from the wind which swept the snow flurries before it. The gale searched through the mill ruin to rattle the ivy leaves and pile drifts against the walls. The owl left his roosting place and flew towards Tacky Bowden's piggery where rats were plentiful among the warm muck heaps. The grey fox shivered and started to uncurl, then, remembering the pain, lay still for fear that the wire would tighten. But a new pain gripped his belly and eventually hunger drove him out.

The iron peg clanked as it dragged over the stones of the clapper bridge. Several times it caught and held fast between rocks or beneath tree roots, and each time the fox's head was jerked back as the wire cut into his neck until he learned to stop at the first hint of obstruction and retrace his steps to free the peg. He was forced to search the ditches and hedge bottoms for worms and insects, but ground life had moved deep into the soil to escape the frost, and the hard surface would not yield to his scratching. He dragged his burden under a field gate, and it slid more easily on the smooth grassland so that he trotted quickly over the two fields to the small paddock where the flock slept. As he poked his snout through a gap in the hedge, the warm smell of newborn lamb reached his nostrils. He tasted the air and licked the saliva from his jowl.

The ewe nuzzled her offspring as it lay half-buried in the snow. She stood over the tiny yellow-stained body as it struggled for life, and she licked the salty taste of natal fluid, massaging warmth into the frail limbs. Suddenly, her head went up as the pungent smell of fox came to her, and she turned in his direction, peering through swirling snow at the unseen menace. The grey fox moved closer and she lowered her head, giving a deep throaty bleat of warning as the grey shape slunk past. Slowly, the fox moved round her while she turned, always to face him, shaking her head and occasionally stamping a foot. Then the pains caught her again and she moved uneasily, distracted by the impending birth of her second lamb. The fox waited, then as the ewe turned for a brief second, he lunged, snatched the lamb and made off as quickly as the iron peg would allow while the robbed matron licked her remaining twin.

On his midnight rounds, Clegg found the ewe and her surviving lamb. From the size, he knew it was one of twins and from the marks in the snow, he also knew where the other lamb had gone. He followed the tracks to the gate, puzzled by the peculiar long groove in the snow. On the bottom of the gate, he found some hairs and examined them by the light of the torch. "That damned grey fox again!" he muttered.

The following night, the fox once more visited the lambing field, but this time all the ewes were safely folded and, although he prowled up and down, he dared not enter for fear of the lowered heads and sharp forefeet of the sheep. In a corner outside the hurdles, he found the afterbirth of a ewe that had lambed earlier in the day, so he took the edge off his hunger with that.

Next morning, Clegg studied the tracks again, and on the third night left hurricane lamps burning outside the pens all night. When the grey fox came, he went away again still hungry and trotted up to Tacky's cottage to scavenge the dustbins. The rattle set Tiger barking so that the old man had to get out of bed to quieten him.

In the morning, Tacky saw the tracks and the long groove in the snow, and guessed what had happened, for he had seen the marks where the missing snare had been pulled out. He had tried to follow the trail, but fresh snow had obliterated it. Now he could see that the animal was dragging the peg, and so would not travel far. He knew that sooner or later it would catch in a tree root or between two boulders and hold firm, and he returned to bed with the satisfying knowledge that within the next few days, he would find the fox dead.

Two nights later, the bins rattled again, and this time Tacky was ready with his twelve-bore beside the bed. Quickly, he lifted the window sash and peered out as Tiger set up a furore of yapping. He fired at a shadow and the pellets peppered the snow round the iron peg, but the grey fox ran on with the peg skittering behind him. He turned up the Ashton road and, avoiding the deep snow on either side, ran up the hard candled wheel marks to the cattle grid. Hesitatingly, he began to walk across, carefully placing each pad on top of the bars. The noise of metal scraping on metal followed him as the iron peg bumped over, and the sound made him stop and turn. He made an effort to jump back to firm ground. There was a click from the direction of the peg, and the wire pulled tight around his neck as the peg wedged beneath the grid bars.

For as long as it took for Tiger to stop barking, the fox lay still, his nose towards the peg. He had learned that pulling caused pain and that retracing his steps freed him from pain. He walked back over the grid, but this time the wire still pulled tight. The pain came again and made him turn and walk again to solid ground where yet again the wire jerked tight, and because he knew no other action, the fox retraced his steps; and so backwards, round and round the peg until black sky softened to grey.

As the first light went on in Tacky Bowden's cottage, the fox heard a click and felt the wire ease on his raw neck. Twice more he walked round, each time further from the peg, and no pain came. Suddenly, he stopped and for a moment studied the frayed end of the wire as it coiled towards him. He pulled back and the end followed him, but the wire did not pull tight. Slowly he turned and, with the weariness of fatigue and hunger, trotted down the hill to seek refuge in the mill ruin.

Three days later, while scratching the half-healed wound on his neck, one hind claw caught in the noose end and, with a quick tug, he was rid of it.

Tacky followed the tracks whenever there were no fresh falls of snow to hide them. Every day he searched, tracing the animal's comings and goings, reading the signs in the snow until he knew every fox path and likely hiding place in the coombe. He found the peg and the wire noose, and knew the fox was free again. More snares were put down and the occasional gin trap, but his quarry had learned to smell out metal and to avoid it, so that after a while Tacky ceased to use them and turned his mind to other methods. He decided to block up all the possible earths during the night so that the fox could not get below ground, then try and flush him out with the terrier during the day and shoot him. It took two nights of hard work to block the holes, and two days after that before Tacky surprised the fox where he slept in a dry hedge bottom. But before the old man saw him, he slipped through the hedge and was gone. Tacky returned the next day but the fox had learned not to kennel in the same place twice.

At night, the stars burned with intense brightness, and aurora borealis blazoned the northern sky. Finches dropped frozen from their perches and the fox crunched their dry, fleshless bodies to swallow nothing but feather and bone. As hunting became more difficult, he foraged the rubbish tip near the village, where half-wild cats, led by a one-eared brindled tom, squabbled and caterwauled over week-old chicken bones. The rats were too big and wily for the strays to catch, but the grey fox caught them and fought the brindled tom for possession. Regularly he prowled the buildings at Ravenscoombe where Clegg lay awake listening to his sheep as they bleated their warnings. He never saw the fox, but he knew he was there, waiting his chance.

It was the third week of frosts, and Tacky stood watching a sow that had farrowed the previous evening. He counted the piglets and scratched his head. "Damned funny," he said to himself. "There were eight last night. I'll swear it." He counted again. "Seven. Now where the 'ell's the other 'un to? 'Ave 'ee laid on 'un? Y'allus were a clumsy ol' sod." But a search of the piggery revealed no crushed piglet. "Couldn't 'ave eaten 'un, 'er's not that sort." He shook his head and walked round to the back of the hut. A line of unmistakable fox tracks led away into the copse. "Bugger me!" yelled Tacky so that Tiger scurried under the nearest pile of timber. "Bugger me," he repeated, "this bloody fox 'ave taken a piglet!"

The old man returned to the cottage and prepared to seek his enemy. He took his poaching bag and his gun, called the terrier and set off to follow the tracks over the road and into Ravenscoombe. As he crossed Lower Brownhill, he met Clegg who, with Skipper, was also looking for the grey fox.

"He's had at least six of my lambs," Clegg told Tacky when he had learned his errand.

"An' a piglet o' mine, from right under th' ol' sow's nose."

"Well, it's getting a bit much now and I want rid of him. Where do you think he'll be?"

Tacky considered for a few moments. "Depends," he said slowly.

"Depends on what?" Clegg asked.

The old man hesitated. "Depends on ow badly 'ee were 'urt by the wire 'ee got into. 'Ee were draggin' the peg about fer days till 'ee got rid of 'un."

"Oh! So that was the odd mark alongside the footprints. I wondered how that came about."

Tacky nodded. "Ah! I nearly got 'un that time for certain." He stopped to break the gun and slip in a cartridge. "Us'd better try the ruins first. I know's 'ee do lay up there sometimes. Th' ol' dog might put 'un out."

Together, the two men crossed the bridge, and when they got within twenty yards of the mill ruin, Tacky called softly to his terrier and slipped a piece of string round the dog's neck. He gave a second piece to Clegg and indicated that he should do the same with Skipper.

"Us don't want 'un to bolt afore we'm ready," he whispered.

Clegg felt strangely elated as they walked towards the mill. A blackbird cackled its warning and Tacky swore under his breath, signalling Clegg to stand still. When the wood had settled again, the old man nodded and they moved on until they had a clear view into the jumble of stones and half-demolished walls, then Tacky handed Tiger's string to Clegg. "Right, my anzum," he whispered, addressing Clegg, "you take the two dogs round to the other side. Tiger'll know what to do if you tell 'un to seek."

Clegg did as he was told, and immediately the terrier dashed into the rubble while the less confident collie followed ten paces behind. High in the ivy, the barn owl launched himself from his roosting place and flapped silently into the wood. For a moment, Tacky raised his gun, then lowered it again and let the bird fly on. Tiger's head and shoulders disappeared beneath the overhang of ivy and the dog began to bark. Once more, Tacky pushed off the safety catch, but only a bewildered rat emerged which Tiger caught, shook, threw over his back and thereafter ignored.

Tacky turned the gun under his arm and shouted to his terrier, "Yer! Good dog! Leave 'un. 'Er's not there." He turned to Clegg. "Us ud better try the quarry. 'Tis likely that's where 'ee's to."

Again, Clegg felt a slight thrill as they moved up towards the badger sett. But the old man shook his head and pointed to the broad long-clawed pad marks of a badger. "Ol' Brock's been about last night, an' 'ee'll 'ave shifted Charlie for certain. They can't abide foxes for long. Foxes is too dirty fer they."

"Who's Charlie?" Clegg asked, half-amused by his companion's dissertation on natural history.

"Why, 'aven't 'ee 'eard folk call a fox Charlie afore? Don't ask why, but 'tis what us 'untin' volk call 'un."

Clegg smiled. The thought of Tacky Bowden as one of the fox-hunting fraternity seemed as unlikely as Huccaby's concern about the ethics of killing wild animals. "I didn't know you were one of Mr Huccaby's supporters," he said.

It was Tacky's turn to grin. "Oh, I enjoys a day with th'ounds. Foller 'um all day I could, on me two-wheeled 'oss." He laughed and Clegg found himself laughing too.

"An' I'll tell 'ee this," Tacky continued. "Us've 'ad a fair few rabbits, 'ar, and pheasants too, that's been put up when 'ounds 'ave run through a covert." He tapped the barrel of his twelve-bore and winked. "Now, us'd better draw up round the ol' quarry to where the stream comes over. 'Ee may be layin' up in they brimbles."

They toiled up the path to send the dogs into the bramble thicket. Immediately both animals began to bark and a half-grown rabbit broke cover. Tacky fired and the rabbit somersaulted to lie kicking in the snow. Clegg was surprised at the old man's quick reaction while Tacky, sensing the younger man's admiration, grinned. "I were reckoned t' be a fair shot in me time," he said as he picked up the body before the dogs emerged from the thicket. He took out his knife and deftly slit open the belly to let the entrails spill on to the snow for the dogs. Then the liver was taken out and the bile duct removed, and finally the liver and heart were put into one of the plastic bags from Tacky's poaching bag. He thrust the knife between the tendons of one hock and pushed the other leg through, and in the same movement handed the rabbit to Clegg. "First o' the day goes to the host," he said with mock formality.

They walked into the open fields and sat on the stone wall that formed the boundary of Ravenscoombe. "You can see the whole valley from yer," Tacky said as he fumbled inside his bag.

Clegg looked down over the smooth fields to the miniature farmhouse and buildings far below, set out like a child's toy in the folds of white bed linen. This was his valley, the real wild place he had always dreamed of, and for one fleeting moment it all seemed worthwhile.

Tacky handed him a thick bacon sandwich. "It'll save 'ee 'aving' t' go back to the 'ouse fer some dinner. T'would be a pity t' spoil a good day's sport fer the want o' grub."

Not without misgivings, Clegg accepted it and was agreeably surprised at the thick salty flavour.

"Made wi' pork drippin' an' best streaky." Tacky confided with his mouth full.

The meal was finished in silence as the men warmed their backs in the noon sun. Both gazed at the familiar landscape with something more than affection. Clegg thought of the old term 'husbandman' and knew that he loved the place as he loved his family; it was like being in love with two women, two women who hated each other.

Tacky handed him the top of a thermos flask filled with hot, sweet tea. The old man was talking. "See that lil' ol' flat field down by the farm, where they lambin' pens is? That's where us used t'break colts a-lungin' an' long reinin'. Then us used t'tie 'um t'thic granite post in the middle, till they were used to bein' tied up, an' little ol' Josh 'ud come an' give us a 'and. Co'rse I'm talkin' about forty odd year ago. Father allus used t'say 'ee were a might too soft with 'un - all right fer the little 'uns mind but father allus used t' give the big 'uns fer me to 'andle. Ah, 'ow time do fly." The old man sighed. "Now this field yer never were no good, but this one by the larches used t' grow good crops, barley an' oats. Bit on the acid side mind, but with a bit o' limestone an' slag 'er would give 'ee a fairish crop."

Tacky rambled on while he waited for his turn with the tea. Clegg for his part began to take notice of what the old man was saying, and he liked the picture he painted of a valley alive with farming activity, of good crops of barley, and flocks of fat sheep. One day it would be like that again, if he had his way.

Tacky suggested they should put the dogs into the gorse and briar patch where he had previously set his snares. "I know 'ee do lay in the furze," he said as he pushed another cartridge into the breech of the shotgun.

The gorse patch yielded only another rabbit for Tacky's poaching bag. "Well, there's only one thing for it. Us'll 'ave t'walk they rocky places at the top o' the coombe," he panted as they began the long climb towards the ridge.

It was half an hour before they eventually reached the top where a clitter of rocks and stones made a formidable shelter for rabbits, badgers and foxes. Tacky brushed the snow from a boulder and sat down to loosen his coat and ease the weight of the bag round his shoulders. "'Tis a maze of a place," he said, "but if th' ol' devil's in there, Tiger'll fetch 'im out. Else us'll 'ave t' dig 'un out."

As he spoke, the terrier set up a frantic yapping and the collie joined in with his deeper bark. A grey shape slipped out from between the boulders and, with a yell, Tacky was on his feet. "Bugger me, there 'ee goes! Yoi! Tally O! Git on 'im, Tiger!" He brought the gun up to his shoulder but was so busy yelling that he left it too late to pull the trigger. By the time he did, the fox was a hundred yards away, dodging between the stones. The kick of the gun caught the old man off balance, his feet slid from under him and he landed on his back in the soft snow, cursing all things and in particular the grey fox. "Git on after 'im!" he hollered as Clegg went to help him to his feet. "Come on! Yoi! Tally O!" Tacky was off down the hill, arms akimbo and his ragged overcoat flapping behind him. The sight was too much for Clegg and nearly helpless with laughter, he tobogganed down the slope on his backside to catch Tacky behind the knees so that both rolled over and over until they came to rest against a gorse clump.

Clegg lay face down, convulsed and breathless, but Tacky was up in a second. "Come on, me anzum!" Yoi! Tally O!" and he was away once more, hatless and covered from head to foot in snow.

Clegg sat on the ground and rocked, tears streaming down his face. "Oh God!" he sobbed. "The Abominable Snowman!" He picked up the old man's hat, knocked the snow off it and jogged after him.

Tacky was standing on the far bank of the Ravensbourne stream when Clegg caught him up. He was looking out over the smooth expanse of Stannon Marsh where, half a mile away, the two dogs were hunting backwards and forwards between the clumps of brown rushes. "Bugger, they've lost 'un," he said wearily as he took his hat from Clegg. "Ah, well! Better luck next time."

Clegg took the heavy poaching bag from off the old man's shoulder and slung it across his own, half-expecting a reproach which never came. They walked in silence, each man with his own thoughts, neither wishing to intrude upon the other's privacy: a comfortable silence borne of shared experience and mutual understanding.

The sun tipped the High Moor as they walked into the yard.

"I'll give 'ee 'an with the jobs," Tacky volunteered with genuine enthusiasm.

"Thank you, I would appreciate that, but we'll have a little something to keep us going first," Clegg answered, leading the way to the house, and Tacky's eyes brightened as he followed.

The old man almost fell into a chair and sat with his gun across his knees without moving. Then he slowly took off his hat, unslung his bag and lay the twelve-bore across the table, broken and showing the empty chamber. "Jist t' remind me not t' forget 'er's not loaded," he told Clegg who was pushing half a tumbler of whisky towards him. He drank most of it in one gulp with a satisfied "Ah!", then wiped the back of his hand across his mouth, topped the rest up with water and sipped it loudly.

He pulled his chair nearer the fire, bending over, elbows on knees, to look into the embers. "Didn' 'ee go though!" he said with such pride that Clegg assumed he was referring to his terrier and muttered something about him being a game little dog.

"No, not 'ee, the grey fox I mean. Wadn't 'ee a beauty, proper grey an' all! By, didn't 'ee go!"

Clegg shrugged and smiled. It was no use trying to sort out this strange love-hate relationship between the hunter and the hunted. Huccaby had certainly got it and he had felt more than a twinge of it himself that day. How illogical could you get? No wonder the deity of the chase was a woman!

They finished the evening chores and Clegg made supper for them both. After the meal, they sat one either side of the fire, and finished the bottle of whisky while Tacky talked of "afore the war" and "when Father were alive" until the clock chimed twelve when he suddenly stood up, put on his hat and bid Clegg good night. Outside the night was cold and the two dogs, who had returned tired and hungry just after dark, wriggled and snorted to be forgiven their absence. Clegg leaned against the doorpost and watched the small figure disappear into the gloom, gun on shoulder and the terrier weaving backwards and forwards at his heels.

He returned to the fire, slumped back into his chair and stretched his legs across the hearth. For the first time for a very long time, he felt almost content. It had been a good day in spite of the grey fox, or was it perhaps because of him? Clegg was too tired to know, but he resolved to write to Cathy. Perhaps this time he would get a reply.

CHAPTER 9

JOSH HUCCABY waited for his alarm to go off, ready to slam it before the noise woke his wife who was breathing heavily in the next bed. He looked over to where she lay. It would be another three hours before Isobel stirred, provided nothing disturbed her in the meantime, and Josh knew better than to do that. The alarm whirred and Josh smothered it before the bell could ring. He waited, but Isobel slept on and he relaxed to contemplate the day's work. The kennels first, then the cattle to see how young Jimmy was shaping up, and finally old John Brimblecombe. The sooner he got the question of the Suffolk rams sorted out, the better.

Josh got out of bed and dressed in the dark, then crept downstairs to wash and shave in the cloakroom where he could make as much noise as he liked. Although it was barely six o'clock, he always made a point of appearing before the men properly shaved and wearing a collar and tie, no matter what the hour. Two cups of strong tea set him up for the morning, and he pulled on his duffle coat and wellingtons and was ready to face the day.

He stepped outside into the blackness and stood for a few seconds to feel the air and listen. He sniffed and a long drawn-out "Ahh!" hung a grey cloud about his lips. The wind had veered and from all directions came the sounds of the melt. "At last," he said with a note of genuine thankfulness. "At last, a thaw."

He drove the half-mile to the kennels and drew into the stone-flagged yard as George Slade, the kennelman, came out of the boiler house, his bare arms red to the elbows with blood.

"Morning, George. I see you've been busy. What is it this time? Someone else's knacker? Not ours, I hope?"

George shook his head. "'Tis an ol' ewe that John Brimblecombe sent down last night. Been dead a while I'd say, but 'er 'ul bile up all right." He swilled his arms under the yard tap. "Tom's wi' the dog-'ounds if you'm lookin' for 'ee."

Josh found Tom Slade in the yard where the dog-hounds exercised.

He was hosing down the granite peeing post that stood in the middle, but as he saw Josh approach, he turned off the water and went to meet him. "Morning, boss."

"Morning, Tom."

Off duty, the young whipper-in had fallen into the habit of referring to the Master as "boss," reserving the more formal "sir" for when he wore hunt livery. Josh had accepted it as a sign of the times and had grown to prefer the more intimate relationship it fostered.

"I s'pose Father has told you we've had another ewe from Higher Ford?"

Josh nodded glumly. "Yes, that's the third in a month." He sighed. "I expect old Brimblecombe has found this weather a bit too much for him and isn't getting round them as he should." As soon as he had said it, he regretted it, for he should not have criticised one member of staff in front of another. "Mind you, he's still the best shepherd this side of Exeter," he added quickly.

The conversation moved to a pleasanter subject for both men as they talked of hounds, and in particular of Warrior. "He's back to his old self," Tom commented as he opened the door to where the hounds lay on their straw-covered benches. All heads raised at the sound of Josh's voice.

"Weya, my good old boys!" he called cheerily, and thirty or more sterns thumped the boards. "Come, Rowdy, come, Portman," he called the dogs by name and they came to him one at a time to come under the Master's critical eye while the whipper-in noted that Roisterous had scabbed an ear, Dawlish had a weeping eye and Yeoman was lame on his near fore.

Finally, Warrior was called. "Good old dog, come on." Josh ran his hand over the muzzle, over his ears and along his ribs to the tail. "No pain there anyway," he commented, "and he moves sound. He'll make the end of the season and then I think we'll use him as a stallion hound. The old chap's got a rare nose and we could do with a bit more of his substance in the pack. Ah, George!" The kennelman had moved up behind his son to peer over his shoulder. "George, we were just saying we'll use Warrior on some of the bitches this year. If I remember rightly, he's out of that Fitzwilliam bitch, Wistful. We'll try him on some of the lighter bitches to get a bit more depth into the next lot of pups."

George agreed, not that it would have been any use to have done otherwise, for he knew that once the 'old man' had set his mind on something, particularly to do with the hounds, heaven and earth wouldn't shift him.

Josh looked at the bitch pack and inspected them with the same care before getting into the Land Rover to drive back to the home farm. It was still dark as he pulled up outside the new concrete and asbestos building where South Devon cattle were being fed silage by the leather-jacketed youth. The main doors were open and the oblong of electric light slanted across the snow to give a clear background to the moving shadows as the boy's head and shoulders crossed and recrossed the beam of light. Inside, the air was warm and thick with the steam of fresh dung and the breath of bawling cattle.

Josh waited until the last forkful had been doled out and the bawling ceased. He studied the big beasts with an approving eye, noting the even covering of flesh under their light brown hides. "As even as peas in a pod," he muttered with satisfaction, then called out to the youth. "They look well, Jim."

The boy looked up and grinned, brushing his long hair back from a red sweating face. "Not so bad, Mr Huccaby, though there's a heifer in there we'd better look at."

"Right, show me which one. A stitch in time … " He was pleased with the boy. Good workers were hard enough to come by, but this one also had his wits about him. Jim led the way into a pen where one animal stood back while the rest pushed and jostled to get at the silage. He went over to her. "It's this one, Mr Huccaby. She's a bit smaller than the rest and I reckon they're knocking her about."

Josh nodded. "Could be," he agreed. "Let's see how she moves."

Jim slapped the animal on the rump with the flat of his hand and she ducked her rump and jumped nervously away.

"She looks bright enough in the eye," Josh continued. "We'll put her into a box and keep an eye on her for a few days."

Together they cleared and littered the isolation box, put the heifer in and stood watching her over the door for a full minute before Josh said, "Let me know how she goes on." The boy nodded and remained watching while Josh returned to the Land Rover. Yes, Josh thought, that lad will make a stockman one day, but I wish he'd get his hair cut!

The vehicle turned out of the gate and down the drive to the road. "Now for Higher Ford," Josh said out loud with a note of anxiety in his voice.

John Brimblecombe was 'mothering on' an orphan lamb as Josh pushed open the gate to the granite and slate cattle hovel that had been divided with hurdles to form eight lambing pens.

"Morning, John," he said as brightly as possible.

"Morning, Master Josh." The old man raised a single gnarled finger to the peak of his cap, as he would have done to Josh's father and grandfather.

"What's this one then?" Josh asked, nodding towards the lamb that John was busily daubing with the remains of the afterbirth from the prospective foster mother.

"'Tis a poor start, I'm afraid, Master. This little 'un were born up over," he nodded towards the moor, "an' us found 'un just in time. Th' ol' ewe were dead a while. But us'll get 'un on to 'ee." He walked over to a half-bred ewe that stood alone in one of the pens. "'Er lost 'er lamb s'morning." He held the ewe's head in the crook of his arm as he knelt beside her and thrust the orphan's nose to her udder, feeling the lamb wriggle as the tiny head butted the ewe's flanks, seeking the nipple amongst the tangle of wool, then the vibrant body relaxed and he knew the milk was flowing into the half-starved lamb. He stayed there holding it for a minute, then pulled the lamb away with a quiet, "There! That's enough for now. Us don't want 'ee a-scourin.'" He straightened his back, resisting the temptation to put a hand where it ached most, and went over to Josh.

"Well, John, I thought I'd see how the half-bred ewes were making out," Josh said as they walked to where the flock was pulling hay from a row of tin and wire racks.

John shook his head. "I don't know, Master Josh, but I don't reckon they'm as 'ard as th'ol' Blackfaces, not by a long chalk."

Josh knew he would have to be patient. "Well, no, John, I don't expect them to be, but these Cheviot Border Leicester crosses will grow better lambs and give us a better clip." He paused for a moment, then continued. "I thought we might try some Suffolk rams up here this autumn. What do you think?"

The response was predictable and Josh was expecting it. The old shepherd shook his head. "Too soft, Master Josh. They sooty-faced beggars 'ud die o' the cold afore Christmas. Nar, there's no beatin' our Dartmoor tups. Let's 'ave none o' they Zuffolks." Josh shrugged his shoulders. He had known it would be difficult but there was plenty of time before October's tupping to work on the old boy. In the meantime, he had four young Suffolk rams growing nicely at Menaridden.

"Will you 'ave a spot o' breakfast?" John asked as they made their way to the long, thatched farmhouse that was the Brimblecombes' home.

"No, thanks, John, I'd better get back for that, but I will pop in and see Polly and have a cup of tea before I go."

The shepherd's face lit up. "Ah, 'er'll be certain glad to zee 'ee. Allus fair tickled t'zee 'er Master Josh, is Polly."

Polly Brimblecombe was frying thick rashers of bacon on a new electric cooker as the two men entered the low-ceilinged kitchen. She hurriedly wiped her hands on her blue-checkered apron and went over to meet them. "Mind your 'ead on that beam, young Master. You'm growed such a girt lad now."

She laughed, and Josh remembered the nursery at the top of the house and the little parlourmaid who was also part nanny. He grinned and held her two brown speckled hands in his and would have liked to hug her as he had as a child when loneliness and fear had driven him from his father's study to seek refuge with Polly and her husband.

"Ah! Do you remember when you and John used to live in the cottage at Menaridden and you used to complain about the old stove?" Josh asked. She nodded. "Well, how do you like this one?" He patted the gleaming enamel as he would a prize horse.

"Why, Josh Huccaby, 'tis a proper job. Mind, 'er takes a bit o' gettin' used to what with this eye level grill thingammy an' all they lil' ol' gadgets. But us'll get used to 'un, even though we'm seventy an' gone."

"I'm sure you will, Polly, the same as John will get used to my new fangled sheep." They laughed, but Polly gave her husband a quick glance with more than a hint of anxiety. "Oh, 'ee will, Master Josh, don't 'ee fret. 'Ee will." She poured the tea and they talked of other things.

It was a grey morning as Josh drove the two miles back to Menaridden and slush spattered the pockmarked snow on the side of the horizon across Ashton Down. The nine o'clock news summary was just finishing as he pulled off his wellingtons and handed his wet coat to Mabel Slade who had put a rasher into the frying pan when she heard the Land Rover draw up.

"Missus 'as 'ad 'ers," she murmured reproachfully, "and you'm late again," she added in the same resigned tone that she used on her husband and son when they were invariably late for meals.

In the dining room, Isobel Huccaby sat in a pink dressing gown at one end of the polished oak table, reading her mail. At the other end, Josh's formidable pile of cellophane windowed bills were placed between his knife and fork. He kissed his wife on the cheek with a mumbled, "Morning, my dear," before pushing the pile of bills into the centre of the table and sitting down. He hid his stockinged feet under the chair as Mabel brought in his breakfast. "It's thawing," he said brightly. "We ought to be able to hunt in a day or two, I thought - "

"I hope you haven't forgotten the Briggs' dinner party tonight," Isobel interrupted with a quick look that intimated she knew he had.

Josh' heart sank. She was right, of course. He had forgotten. "Well, er ... " He groped for an excuse not to go. "The problem is ... " he said slowly, "we've got a sick heifer and I may have to call the vet in and you know he rarely gets round to us before evening unless it's an emergency." He thought that sounded convincing and got on with his meal. "I can't afford to lose her," he added, eyeing the pile of bills in front of him.

But Isobel was not convinced. "It's always the same with you. If it's not a sick cow, it's a lame horse. You're getting to be the most unsociable man in the county. Surely you could put yourself out for one evening. After all, the Briggs are the wealthiest subscribers in the hunt." She paused for a moment and then added with vehemence, "At least they can pay their bills on time!"

Josh concentrated on his breakfast. He had to admit that the Briggs' chain of supermarkets was indeed lucrative, but Briggs he considered was a stuck-up snob who hunted only because he fancied himself as a country squire, and Mrs Briggs' loud voice with its assumed ultra-refined accent set his nerves on edge. No, an evening cooped up with that pair was just not on.

"And Colonel Waters will be there," Isobel continued.

Gin-swilling old bore, Josh thought.

"And Mrs Crawthorn."

Oh God, not her!

He put his knife and fork down, took a deep breath and said, "Well, I'm not going. I'll ring 'em up this morning."

Isobel stood up. "Well, I'm going, and I'm sure Reggie Waters will be only too pleased to escort me." She swept out and banged the door behind her.

Josh buttered his toast. "Well, that's settled then," he said out loud, and then a little louder, "I hope the old blighter stays sober enough to drive home." He sighed and looked out of the window to check that the snow was really going. Yes, the mist was lifting and there was a light drizzle. It was going to be a quick thaw. They would want to draw the Briggs coverts as soon as the snow went, and Briggs did own Trenden Wood which they would have to draw to find the grey fox for the Ravenscoombe chap. "All right, I'll go!" he yelled. "After all," he said quietly to himself, "I may be able to get away early."

After breakfast, the stables were always a cheerful sight with the horses tacked up ready for exercise and Jenny, the groom, bustling around, her ample form stretching faded blue jeans to bursting point. "I'll ride with you today!" Josh called cheerily. "It'll do me good after the inactivity of the past weeks."

Jenny smiled and whispered to the chestnut she was grooming, "Hallo, sure sign the weather's breaking. The boss has come to life again and you'll be hunting within the week."

Josh was looking over the loose box door. "We'll grease their heels to keep the snow from balling. We have got studs in them all, I suppose? I'll take Grizzle." The questions and orders rattled out without any pause for reply, and Jenny looked at the chestnut and winked while Josh went next door to pull up the girths and lengthen the stirrup leathers of the blue roan mare.

Grizelda was a big Irish hunter renowned for her sure-footedness and bad temper. She humped her back and lay back her ears as Josh settled in the saddle, but he kept a tight hold of her head to prevent her bucking, at the same time growling under his breath, "Goorron, y'damned old fool!" Stiff-legged, she danced out of the yard, peering at anything that moved, as though looking for an excuse to play up, while her rider chuckled and gave her no chance. They knew each other very well.

They trotted up the lane and on to the moor where a well-marked track gave the opportunity for a canter. We'll risk it, Josh thought as he felt the ground give under the softening snow. He squeezed the mare with his knees and eased the reins. He heard her snort as she pulled at the snaffle, and felt the cold air sharp against his cheeks as she lengthened her stride to increase the pace. Josh took a deep breath and felt good. He looked back to see Jenny on the chestnut, her face glowing and blonde hair streaming out behind, and he thought of Isobel and the daughter they might have had, and was glad he had agreed to go to the dinner party.

They rode to the Ashton Ridge above Ravenscoombe and looked down to where a lone oilskinned figure moved slowly among the small flock of sheep, carrying bales of hay from barn to field. "Rather him than me," Josh murmured, then wondered if he really meant what he was saying. Perhaps his feeling was one of envy: envy of the man's solitude and freedom. "It must be nice to be able to do what you like when you like," he said to Jenny as they turned their horses towards home. The girl grinned sheepishly and nodded.

By the time they reached Menaridden, the roads were black shining rivers and every gully was a bubbling turmoil of brown water. By mid-afternoon, the water meadows below Colspit Wood were a shallow lake with floating islands of slush and dead sticks. In Ashton, they piled sand bags in the doorways of shops and watched anxiously the flood marks on the bridge. Josh was tempted to use this as an excuse not to go to the dinner party but decided against it. Instead he had an earnest conversation with Jimmy, tucked a pound note into the boy's top pocket and returned to the house with the satisfaction of knowing that at least his stay at the Briggs' would not be unduly prolonged.

They arrived at The Barton, the Briggs' residence, half an hour late, for at seven o'clock Jenny had looked in to say that Grizelda was lame and Josh had insisted on going up to the stables, dinner jacket and all, to inspect the trouble and help the girl poultice the near-fore tendon.

Meanwhile, Isobel sat in her fur coat and drummed the kitchen table. She had known this sort of situation to last two hours. It was therefore with some relief that she found herself only half an hour late, with their hosts just hovering over the soup debating whether or not to order it to be served.

"Just in the nic-o-tine, as the tobacconist said!" Briggs called out as they entered the hall, and Isobel smiled weakly. Josh did not understand why Briggs was guffawing and so grinned as affably as he could in case there was a joke he had missed. He always missed Briggs' jokes.

During dinner, it occurred to Josh that his host was less insufferable than usual while Mrs Briggs was more so. God, how he hated horseywomen. Perhaps, he reflected, that was why he had married Isobel, refined, sophisticated Isobel, the darling of the tennis club. That was ten years ago, at a time when most people had thought he would settle for permanent bachelordom. He had been forty and she twenty-five. He glanced across the table to where an animated Isobel was obviously enjoying herself discussing politics with a watery-eyed Colonel Waters. Josh smiled. Yes, he was glad he had come now. He caught her eye and she smiled back. Yes, he was very glad.

Mrs Crawthorn, next to him, was holding forth on the despoiling of Dartmoor by the planting of conifers, a favourite hobby horse of hers and one which she rode with much emotion and scant regard for fact. Josh glanced at his watch. Twenty-five past nine. He sat back while the dessert plates were cleared away by a girl he recognised as a waitress from the Tudor Tea Rooms in Ashton. Brandy and liqueurs were brought in and Josh knew that the next thing would be that Briggs would suggest was a game of cards, and Josh hated cards. He was no good at it and invariably embarrassed his partners and Isobel into the bargain. At nine thirty, the telephone rang in the hall and Josh gave a visible sign of relief. He glanced around the room. Isobel and Mrs Briggs were deep in conversation and hardly noticed when Briggs tiptoed over to him and said, "It's for you."

He walked towards the door and in response to an inquiring look from Isobel, touched her shoulder and said quietly, "Don't worry. It's probably Jimmy about the heifer." With a satisfying click, he closed the thick buzz of talk and tobacco behind the solid oak door and picked up the telephone. "Well done, Jimmy. Everything all right? Good."

He replaced the receiver and waited for a few moments before returning to the party. "Sorry but I'll have to leave you," he told his host. "Problems with a sick animal, you know. No need for Isobel to come. I'll fix up a taxi to fetch her."

Mrs Briggs stalked over. "That won't be at all necessary, my dear Mr Huccaby. Isobel is very welcome to stay here for the night, what with these beastly floods."

Josh said he was grateful, and, fetching his hat and coat, kissed Isobel on the cheek and, with considerable alacrity, made for the door.

Outside the fine drizzle had turned to rain and Josh began to wonder whether the ensuing floods would further curtail his hunting. He reminded himself to pay a call on Granger, and on impulse decided to do it then and there. He stopped at the King's Head and bought a bottle of whisky, with the thought that he could at least offer the chap a drink for all his trouble over Warrior and the grey fox.

CHAPTER 10

CLEGG FINISHED his letter and read it once more before scrawling his name on the bottom. He looked at it for a moment, then hastily added two crosses, folded it and sealed it in the envelope, to which he added a stamp. There! It's done, he thought as he placed it on the window sill under the back porch where the postman would be sure to pick it up. As he did so, a pair of headlamps swung off the main road and on to the farm drive. He stood and watched them swing to and fro as the vehicle took the steep bends, and he wondered what sort of lost traveller could possibly be calling at that time of night. The large car pulled up in the yard and he was surprised to see the tall figure of Josh Huccaby step out.

"I was just on my way home and I thought I would drop in to say that we shall be meeting at the King's Head a week on Tuesday and I would like to draw the coombe if that's all right with you?"

Clegg opened the door wide and indicated that Josh should enter. Inside, Josh stood for a moment or two, then unbuttoned his overcoat, took out the bottle of whisky from his inside pocket and placed it on the table. Clegg smiled inwardly at the sight of the starched shirt and black bow tie. It was a long time, he reflected, since he had worn his, and that occasion had ended in a stand-up row with Cathy's father.

His visitor was still speaking: " ... I've had you on my conscience for some time and I wondered if you would accept this as a token of my appreciation for looking after my hound, and as a little compensation for your battered roof."

Clegg walked over to the fire and poked it. "That's very kind of you," he said. He moved to the dresser and put two glasses on the table. "Water? I'm afraid there's no soda."

Josh nodded, took off his overcoat and settled into a chair next to the fire. Clegg handed him his drink and sat down in the armchair on the other side of the fireplace.

It was Josh who spoke first. "I haven't been in this room for over twenty years," he said, looking around. "It must have been just after the old man Bowden died." He sipped his whisky and turned back to the fire. There was a long pause before he continued. "He was a hard man, but a damned good farmer."

Clegg nodded, and Josh thought hard for something else to say but could only follow with a loud "Hmmm!", then lapsed into silence.

Suddenly, a shot close to the house caused Skipper to squirm to his feet and bolt for the door, barking furiously. Both men sat up in their chairs and looked at each other as the collie's bark was answered by a yap, followed by scratching outside. Clegg moved quickly to the door and opened it a few inches. A wet, bedraggled Tiger squeezed past and made for the fire, and a moment later Tacky Bowden's voice sounded from across the yard. "All right, 'tis only me."

Clegg pushed the door wide open so that the broad beam of light shone across the wet flags and on to the small overcoated figure. Tacky was obviously pleased with himself. "I've got 'un, for certain I've got 'un. Peppered 'un good an' proper, I did. 'Ee were just along o' your orchard an' ... " He stopped in mid-sentence as he crossed the threshold and saw Josh standing by the fire. For a second, he was nonplussed, and Clegg could not make out whether it was the dinner jacket or the fact that he was obviously confessing to the crime of fox shooting in front of a Master of Foxhounds.

For once, Tacky was at a loss for words, but the lapse was only momentary. "Why, Josh, I never thought to see you yer. 'Tisa poor night to be out, an' you'm all dressed up an' all." As he spoke, he propped his gun in the corner by the sink. "I were just callin' on Mr Granger to say as I've settled a little account for 'un." He winked confidentially at Clegg as he took off his hat and prepared to make himself at home.

Clegg looked from Tacky to Josh. It was the Master of the Foxhounds' turn to speak. "Unless I'm greatly mistaken, Thomas Ackland Bowden, you have been shooting my foxes again." The tone was severe, but Clegg noticed the flicker of a smile across the tanned face.

Tacky was undaunted by the show of authority, and it occurred to Clegg that they had played this game before. "I didn't know they were your foxes," the old man retorted. "An' in any case, you don't seem to catch any wi' they bloody ol' 'ounds o' yours."

"We've killed twenty brace this season already." Josh appeared indignant.

"Twenty brace!" Tacky snorted. "Twenty brace! All that chasin' about wi' expensive 'osses an' a girt pack of 'ounds just t' kill forty foxes. Why, that wouldn't make no difference to nothin'. All you does, Josh Huccaby, is to keep they foxes well exercised an' fit so as they can give 'ee a good run."

"And I suppose you think your shooting and snaring is a better way of going about it?"

"Well, at least I don't 'ave to spend thousands o' pounds an' get all dressed up to do it."

"Thomas Ackland, you're a cantankerous old cuss."

"No, I bain't and you know it."

At that point, Clegg judged the honours slightly in the old man's favour and offered him a generous helping of whisky to indicate that the contest was over.

Tacky pulled up a chair and stretched his legs forward until his wellington boots steamed. "Ah," he said appreciatively, "there's nothin' like a good fire."

Josh chuckled quietly and settled back into his chair. "Well, you're quite your old self again. We haven't had a really good argument since you gave up Ravenscoombe. What's got into him, Mr Granger?"

Clegg shrugged and grinned at Tacky. "I suppose you might say that Mr Bowden has become my technical adviser, particularly on the question of vermin control."

"You mean he's been shooting foxes."

"'Er's got a one-track mind," Tacky interjected.

Clegg poured more liquor before the argument could start again, then turned to face the old man. "And is it true you've shot the grey fox?"

"Ar!" There was a note of defiance in the utterance. "Anyways, us peppered 'un good an' proper, as I said. I seed 'un jump a foot in the air afore 'ee dropped into the ditch, but 'tis a maze o' brimbles an' I couldn't see 'un. Er's dead as mutton for certain." He stared into the fire and bent down to stroke the terrier at his feet. "Yes," he said quietly, "dead for certain."

Josh grunted and drained his glass, while Clegg said nothing lest he betray his anger: anger that a wild thing was dead, anger that he had been party to it, anger that he had enjoyed the hunt in the snow.

Tacky sighed, a long drawn-out "Ahhh!" which had little satisfaction in it. "'Tis all over then." He pulled the dog's ears. "Us'll 'ave no more trouble from 'ee."

"Are you sure you killed him?" Josh asked. "You know how difficult it is to stop a full-grown fox, and it wouldn't be right to leave the poor brute lying half-dead in the ditch to crawl away and die of lead poisoning. I reckon we ought to go and look for it, if only to put it out of its misery. I still think you shouldn't have shot it."

Tacky prickled again. "Why, damn it, man, 'e were a lamb killer."

"Well, let's not start that all over again," Clegg said as he topped up the glasses.

They drank in silence as the clock's hollow tick-tock measured the seconds, each man thinking his own thoughts about the grey fox.

Clegg was the first to speak. "Well, if we're going to look for it, we'd better go. I'll lend you a pair of boots, Huccaby." They emptied their glasses and, none too steadily, assembled at the back door to "tack up fer the weather" as Tacky put it.

Clegg led the way to the orchard, swinging the beam of his big torch across the grey wall of mist that clung to the lichen-covered branches. The other two followed in silence except for the occasional "Christ, 's dark!" from Tacky as he stumbled over dead branches.

At the top, Clegg stopped and handed the torch to the old man who led them to a clump of brambles by the boundary wall. "'Er's in the bottom o' that lot o' brimbles," he said, shining the torch into the thick tangle. "I seed 'un drop off that wall."

Josh picked up a half-rotten fence post. "Then I shall have to knock 'em down and find the late lamented remains of Charles James Fox," he said, blinking hard before commencing to flail the brambles with the post.

The flailing ceased while Josh removed his overcoat and unbuttoned his dinner jacket; at the same time, Tacky took the opportunity to grab both dogs in order to prevent the Master of Foxhounds from inadvertently murdering them. Josh returned to his work with renewed vigour, and as he flung back his arms for a final swing, the top six inches of the post detached itself and landed on Clegg's chest with sufficient force to unbalance his stance already made unsteady by the whisky. He landed on his back in the long grass and felt strangely disinclined to get up.

Josh paused, knee-deep in his bramble patch, to mop his forehead with his white silk scarf. "Where the hell's Granger gone?" he asked, swaying forward and propping himself up with the fence post. "Just when things are warming up, the damned feller goes and disappears. God, it's warm! Granger, where are you?" He turned to where Tacky stood clutching the scruffs of the two dogs. "Well, don't just stand there, Tacky Bowden. Bring those two damned cur dogs down here and let's see what's what."

Tacky let the dogs go with a hoarse, "Seek 'un! Gud dog, seek 'un!"

The terrier pushed eagerly into the tangled briars and could be heard snuffling and growling to himself. Suddenly, he set up a furious barking which caused his owner to start down the bank yelling, "Gud ol' Tiger! Well done, my booty! 'Ee've found 'un! Oh, bloody 'ell!" The last as his wellingtons slid from under him and he landed on his backside in the sodden ditch.

Clegg scrambled to his feet and propped himself against the wall. "What's s'matter?" he asked, still dazed.

"We've got him!" Josh called, bending down to thrust an arm into the brambles in the direction of the barking. "I can feel him!" and then in a quieter voice, "He's dead as mutton."

He pulled the body out and threw it at Clegg's feet. Tacky pulled himself out of the ditch and shone the torch down, and the three men stared at the bedraggled corpse of a large one-eyed brindled cat.

Tacky dropped on to one knee. "'s a bloody cat," he said incredulously. "'s a bloody cat," he repeated louder, grinning up at his companions. "'s not the lill' ol' grey fox at all." He began to giggle uncontrollably. "Well, I'll be damned ... us 'ave shot a bloody cat!"

Josh laughed and picked the remains up by the tail with a loud whoop. Through the haze of alcohol, it occurred to Clegg that a half-wild cat came very low on their list of favourite things. "Does it belong to anybody?" he asked in an attempt to curb their hilarity.

Josh paused for a moment and thought. "Perhaps it's one of Mrs Wrightson's," he beamed.

Tacky snorted and gave a loud "Ha!", and Clegg gathered that the lady was even lower on the list of favourite things. "Who's Mrs Wrightson?" he asked.

Josh picked up his overcoat and slung it over his shoulder before replying. "Mrs Wrightson, my dear chap, is the bane of my life. She came to live in Ashton from somewhere upcountry, London, I think, about two years ago. She is anti-everything: hunting, forestry, battery hens, sprays. You name it, she's ag'in it. The only thing she's for is cats, and she's got dozens of those, but I shouldn't think this feller is one of 'em. He's not fat enough." He held the cat out at arm's length. "No, this one's a wild 'un, and since it's not one of Mrs W's," he added more brightly, "we'll give it a decent burial." So saying, he led the way, cat still held out in front of him, down the hill towards the farm.

Clegg found a spade and they laid the brindled tom to rest in a recently cleared patch in the kitchen garden. The three men stood, somewhat unsteadily, round the fresh mound of earth, then Josh snatched Tacky's battered hat from his head and thrust it into his hands. "You shot it. Y'might at least show a bit of respect."

Tacky mumbled inaudibly and crammed the even more crumpled hat back on to his bald pate as the rain gusted round the corner of the house.

Clegg shivered. "Let's get inside," he said. "I could do with a drink."

Inside the kitchen, the pressure lamp burned yellow and low. Clegg poked at the fire while the other two arranged their wet coats along the backs of the chairs. The last of the whisky was poured out, amounting to half a tumblerful each, then they sat back to soak up the warmth while the two wet dogs squeezed through outstretched legs to lie steaming in front of the hearth.

Josh was the first to speak. "Funny about it being a grey fox," he said with a sideways glance at Tacky.

"Why?" asked Clegg. "I thought we had agreed that a grey fox was by no means unheard of."

"Nar," Tacky growled. "'Er's on about the Ackland fox. 'Tisa lot of ol' rubbish but 'er makes a gud yarn. You tell 'un, Josh."

The MFH took a long sip of whisky, put the glass on the table and eased himself into a more comfortable position in his chair. "Well, the story goes something like this," he began. "It all started with old Tacky's great-grandfather. He was quite a character: owned most of the land between Ashton and the moor, one of the old school. Anyway, he was Master of this pack and hunted them himself, as I do. Well, not exactly as I do, by all accounts a damned sight better. Where was I? Ah, yes. Well, the old boy was drawing the woods where the new conifer plantation is now when suddenly he hollered a fox away at the far end, yelling back to his whipper-in that a grey fox had gone away. Now the strange thing was that the whip, who was not far behind, swore that he saw no fox and that the hounds would not own the line even when the old man hollered them on. Anyway, off they went, the Master doubling his horn and calling his hounds on, and a bewildered whip following on, wondering whether or not his boss had finally gone round the bend. They soon left the rest of the field and swung in a wide arc, some say fifteen miles as hounds run, crossing the river by Stoneycombe Cleave and ending up at Hods Barrow, the old stone circles beyond Trenden Hill. According to the whip, whose name I've forgotten - "

"Jack Gliddon," Tacky interjected.

"Ah, yes, Jack Gliddon. Well, he was about half a mile behind, his horse being pretty blown, and he told my grandfather afterwards that he could see the old man on the skyline a-whooping and hollering with his hounds clustered round him. He thought they had killed, but when he reached them, there was no sign of a fox. Well, to cut a long story short, Gliddon got the old boy home where he was promptly put to bed. Next morning he - Gliddon, that is - was walking past the front of the house at about six o'clock on the way to the kennels when he heard a fox scream, and sure enough, there in the middle of the lawn, sat a big grey fox staring up at the one lit bedroom window. Gliddon walked across the drive to get a better look, but the fox had gone. Just at that moment, one of the parlourmaids runs out and told him that the Master had that minute breathed his last."

Josh paused for the maximum dramatic effect and then added, "Oh, of course, I forgot to say the old gentleman's name was Thomas Ackland, the same as our illustrious friend here." He nodded towards Tacky.

"Load o' rubbish," Tacky grunted, leaning forward to move a log further into the flames.

"But you must admit that a grey fox has been considered an omen of bad luck ever since. Aren't they supposed to have seen one before the old house caught fire and again just before the Acklands finally went bust in the thirties? I'll tell you this, I bet there was an old grey fox about when the Acklands married into the Bowden family."

Josh grinned and winked at Clegg, and Tacky made a noise so like a growl that Tiger's hackles rose.

"Don' 'ee start on about my folks. They were as good as yorn, Josh 'uccaby, an' at least my father 'ad more sense than to buy one 'orse twice in the same day, which is more'n can be said fer yorn. 'Ave 'ee 'eard that one, Granger?"

"I'm called Clegg at home," Clegg replied, "but go on."

"Well, then, young Clegg, 'twere like this. When Josh's father were about your age, 'ee were a master man to swank an' used to drive a pair o' matched 'orses in tandem. Proper smart turnout, it were. 'Ee won prizes at Olympia 'tween the wars with 'un. Course, the 'uccabys 'ad more money 'n they knew what to do with then. Still 'av." He shot a glance at Josh who sat with closed eyes, his face expressionless.

Tacky continued. "Us used to do a few odd jobs for 'un, an' one day 'ee came over to our place an' says to me, 'Bowden,' 'ee says, 'Bowden, I'd like you to come along with me to Four Lanes fair. I expect to buy a horse and would like you to bring it home for me.' Well, I were only a bit of a lad an' glad to go, fer it were a master place fer a good time wi' the fair an' the 'orse-dealin', not to mention the maids. Course, the place were alive with gyppos an' travellers an' you 'ad to keep tight 'old of yer wallet. Anyway, us puts up at the Bull an' goes to look round the 'orses afore the auction starts. Y'see in them days more deals were done outside the auction ring than in it. Well, us goes into the field an' there coming towards us were a gyppo-looking' chap leadin' a rare girt bay 'orse full sixteen two wi' white socks behind. Us didn' go straight up, o' course, but a few minutes later just strolled over casual. Soon as us showed interest, the gyppo starts trottin' th'orse up an' down. After a bit of 'agglin', 'uccaby buys 'un, an' I must say 'ee were a good sort of 'orse, rough in 'is coat, it being wintertime, an' with a long mane an' a tail as nearly touched the ground, just as though 'ee'd been brought up straight out of the field. 'Take 'im back to the Bull,' 'ee says to me, 'an' 'ere's something for you to spend while I look for another as near like 'im as I can find,' an' 'ee gave us five shillin'. With that, the gyppo says 'ee knowed of the spitten image o' this 'orse about a mile away an' if I got back in ten minutes, 'ee'd take us to un'. Well, I gets back an' the gyppo says we'm to 'ave a drink wi' 'im to clinch the deal. 'uccaby weren't so keen, but 'ee were set on seein' this other 'orse, so we went to the other pub - the only one that would serve gyppos - an' starts in on the whisky.

"I reckon 'twere over an hour afore us got away, an' then the gyppo 'ad to 'arness a skewbald mare to a gig, an' off us went, up narrow green lanes, along by the railway, over to some woods. I reckon us were goin' round in circles. 'Owesome us come to some farm buildin's an' there were this 'orse in a loose box, an' true enough 'ee were very like the one us'd just bought 'cept'n 'ee were smarter, all clipped out, wi' a 'ogged mane which means shaved right off, an' a shorter tail, but only one white sock, on 'is near hind. 'uccaby were quite taken an' in no time at all 'ad bought this'n from the London sort o' chap as owned 'im. Well, us came back to the fairground a lot quicker than us went, an' the gyppo disappeared a might sharp. When us got back to the Bull, the box was empty an' the landlord says as 'ow a 'uccaby's groom'd collected the animal more'n two hours since. Course the other hind pasturn soon grew out white again but the gyppo an' the London chap were never found. An' that's 'ow this yer Master o' Fox 'ounds' father bought the same 'orse twice."

Tacky sat back with a satisfied chuckle that wheezed into a convulsive cough and left him purple-faced.

After that, there was another long silence during which it slowly dawned on Clegg that he was expected to make a contribution. He realised that he already knew a great deal about Tacky and Josh and he had not returned the compliment. But he had no common ground from which to draw his expected tale. There was nothing that these two men might be interested in, so he stared fixedly at the fire and said nothing.

It was Josh who turned the conversation back to the one subject that concerned all three: the grey fox. "Y'know, I'm damned relieved you didn't get that fox, aren't you, Clegg?"

Clegg nodded, and Josh went on. "Interesting how the grey colouring crops up every now and again. They say that in the eighteen-sixties, a lot of foxes were brought down from Scotland and the North to keep the numbers up in the Shires and that many of the grey ones stem from those. Do you see many in the North, Clegg?" It was a shot in the dark, but Josh had detected a slight northern accent and the name was Scottish.

Clegg looked thoughtful. "My grandfather once mentioned a grey tod, as they call them in Scotland, but I spent very little time on the farm so I wouldn't know. Y'see, my father left for the South before I was born so I only spent my holidays there, just enough to get it into my blood, you might say." He paused. It was a long pause during which he looked from Josh, who had settled back with his eyes half-closed, to Tacky and back again. The old man nodded with an encouraging "Hmm," as though anticipating a long and interesting tale, so Clegg fixed his gaze on the shapes in the fire and began.

He told them about his boyhood and his memories of the farm overlooking the Tay, of his time at sea as a junior officer on a cruise liner, and how he met Cathy on the Adriatic Star, and how they were married three weeks later.

It was as though the floodgates of his mind, long shut, had been prised open, so that the thoughts, hopes and fears poured out. "They made me leave the sea." He pushed a log with his toe. "Not Cathy - her people. Gave me a job in their plastics firm in Southampton." He looked up and stared Tacky full in the face. "I was responsible for the sales of the garden ornaments department." He frowned. "You know, plastic gnomes and things."

The old man's face crinkled very slightly, the corners of his mouth twitched and he coughed.

"You know," Clegg grinned, "I was really quite good at it."

"An' what made 'ee decide t' come farming?" Tacky asked.

Clegg thought for a while. "I can remember the exact minute," he said slowly. "I'd never really hit it off with Cathy's father, but I had been grateful for the chance of making a decent living. By that time, we had Stephen and a nice house by the sea, and I even had a small cabin cruiser, Seadrift, we called her, so we could get away from people once in a while. But in spite of it all, I wasn't really happy. Somehow I couldn't feel a complete man doing the job I was doing, and more and more I thought of getting back to basics, of growing food, tending stock. More and more I wanted to return to the way of life I had known as a boy on my grandfather's farm. It had all seemed so good then. After my parents split up, I used to look on it as home ... " He stopped again to contemplate the fire.

"Yes, I remember well," he resumed. "We had all been summoned to the old man's table for a sort of family dinner party, black ties and all. Besides Cathy and me, there were the two sons and their wives, and a cousin who had recently returned from the United States. After the meal, the old man calmly announced that they had decided to open a new factory in Croydon and that I would be joining the staff there to work under this cousin. That was the minute I decided to quit and go farming. He hadn't even had the decency to ask me beforehand, just assumed I would do his bidding as everyone else did. Well, he didn't own me, and I told him so, and that was that. We sold up all we had, and I bought this place."

"And your wife stood by you in this?" Josh asked.

Clegg nodded. "Oh, yes." He thought for a moment. "Now I look back on it, it took some guts to come out of a town into a place like this." He ran his eyes over the kitchen and sighed. "But it was too much in the end. You can't blame her. There was Stephen to think about."

"An' where's 'er to now then?" Tacky queried.

Clegg shrugged and frowned. "I haven't heard from them for over a month except for a couple of postcards. The last one was postmarked London." He tailed off the last sentence as though talking to himself.

The pressure lamp spattered and went out, leaving the dying fire to flicker its yellow lit shadows around the room. Skipper yawned and slowly scratched a flea behind his left ear.

Josh grunted. "It's not easy for a woman," he said, "particularly if she comes from the town." He thought of Isobel in her party frock, and suddenly felt ashamed of the way he had engineered his early departure from the Briggs house. "No, it's not easy for them," Josh repeated quietly.

"No," Clegg echoed.

The ash log sparked with a sudden crackle, sending a shower of light into the gloom, but neither man nor animal stirred. The clock whirred and struck once.

"Well, I must be going," Josh said suddenly, pulling himself out of the chair and groping for his overcoat. "Come on, Tacky, I'll give you a lift. Thanks for your company, Clegg. I've enjoyed it." He gave Tacky a nudge. "Come on, you old reprobate, or we'll never get home."

Clegg led the way to the door, murmuring his thanks for the whisky. Outside, the air was chill, and Tacky puffed his cheeks and coughed as the cold bit into his lungs. Clegg watched the old man trundle after Josh with Tiger close at his heels. He stood in the doorway while the car revved and skidded up the slush-covered track.

The sound faded and the night was silent save for the sounds of the melt. Clegg felt as though a great weight had been lifted from his shoulders, and, as he turned to go in, far down the coombe, a fox barked.

CHAPTER 11

IN TWENTY-FOUR HOURS of thaw, the Ravensbrook swelled from a tumbling stream to a roaring torrent, bowling rocks the size of footballs along its course like peas down a grain chute. On the flat land below the farm, it spread out, before swirling with silent power between the steeper sides of Colspit Wood and thrashing itself into spray and spume over the stone slabs of the clapper bridge. Below the wood, it broadened once more to cover the water meadows and give the river Asher the breadth it had had when the great elk grazed its marshes, and bear and wolf prowled the oak forest along its banks.

Four days it rained, while cattle that had withstood the bitter cold frosts and thrived, now stood humpbacked and dull-eyed in the shelter of hedge banks. On the High Moor, the black hornless Galloways squelched through the seas of mud to reach the in-by land where hay was scattered. Pony mares, large-bellied with next year's foals, stood with heads down, their long, ragged tails plastered to their quarters by the gale.

The farmland soaked up the rain so that the top spongy turf of old pastures oozed moisture at every cloven hoof print. New leys were poached until dairy cows stood hock-deep, and cowmen cursed the mud while they tended hardened udders and chapped teats. Even the hardy sheep stopped grazing and huddled together in tight bunches, waiting for the rain to stop. Clegg picked up a dead ewe and three dead lambs in one night, while the grey fox found a fourth lamb drowned in a gully and carried it back to the cluster of rocks at the head of the coombe where he had kennelled day and night during the deluge.

As curling mist tumbled over the ridge of the High Moor to hang, like wisps of smoke in the top most branches of the Ravenscoombe oaks, Clegg battled with the water. It poured off the hillside behind the farm to gouge a channel two feet wide between the big stones of the yard, and it came up through the rat holes in the shippon and soaked the cattle food, while inside the house the wallpaper in the disused living room crinkled in dark patches as the damp seeped into the cob walls.

As daylight faded on the fourth day, the wind dropped and shifted two points to the south. The confused cloud layers were teased apart like grey cotton wool where ragged holes held the first glint of starlight. Tentacles of mist swirled and disappeared until only the highest rocks of Cragg Tor were held as the rain stopped.

The grey fox squeezed out from his couch between the stones and stretched. He was cold and hungry and ran quickly to the rim of the High Moor to stand, one forefoot raised, scenting the night air. A pale disc of moon suddenly brightened as the sky cleared, turning the gullies and streams to quicksilver. In the coombe, a wood owl hooted to be answered by another beyond the Ashton road. The fox's sensitive ears picked out the night sounds above the roar of the stream as it foamed through the cleft and cascaded into the coombe. He moved a pace forward, then, as though suddenly making up his mind, he flicked his brush and made for Trenden Wood at a steady lope.

He paused on a piece of kale stubble to take the edge off his appetite with a few large earthworms, brought to the surface by the rising water. In Trenden Wood, he hunted the eagerly feeding rabbits until his hunger was satisfied, then he hunted them for pleasure from Trenden to Colspit. As the rising sun drew the mists from the ground, he ran down to the flooded water meadows and gorged on voles drowned in their burrows beneath the tangle of long grass. Belly now filled, he found a dry couch in the hollow bowl of a wych elm and curled up to sleep.

The sun rose into a clear sky, and catkins nodded to a breeze that stirred the last purple leaves in the bramble thicket. The hen buzzard courted the thermals to wheel and turn in an ever-widening spiral, higher and higher until she was a tiny cruciform speck against the endless blue. The water that lapped the roots of the wych elm gradually sank into the leaf mould and was gone, leaving rotting vegetation to steam in the new warmth. A grey wagtail fluttered delicately across the fresh mud in search of insects, cocking his long tail to keep balance on the protruding twigs, and a pair of moorhens chucked and quarked as they fossicked among the reed clumps.

The fox started as a heron called and flapped into the air on heavy tipped wings. Footsteps squelched across the sodden pasture and the sound of men's voices came on the wind. He tensed, ready to run, but the danger passed on down the valley. A dog barked in the distance, too far to cause alarm, so he relaxed again and dozed.

Clegg called Skipper to be quiet as he watched the two men leave their yellow Land Rover and pace over the meadow, carrying bundles of red and white poles and a tripod. He saw them make sightings and bore for soil and rock samples. "Old Briggs must be going to put in a drainage scheme," he told the dog. "It won't work, though. There's not enough outfall. Still, he's got plenty of money." He patted the collie's ribs and received an enthusiastic face lick in return.

The men disappeared into a stand of oak coppice where the two sides of the valley curved inwards to form a narrow cleave. He waited with the thought of asking them what was going on, but they did not reappear, and in any case, he reasoned, the land belonged to Briggs, so what he did was his own business. He decided to leave them to it.

When Clegg returned to the farm, Josh was waiting in the yard.

"Morning, Clegg."

"Morning, Josh."

They greeted each other like old friends.

"We've put off the King's Head meet for a week," Josh said cheerily. "I thought I'd better let you know. The ground's much too wet and we'd do a hell of a lot of damage galloping across these fields. I'm taking hounds up on to the moor out of harm's way instead." He looked around the yard. "How's the lambing going? Had any more trouble?"

Clegg shook his head. "Not from our foxy friend. Just the usual rotten luck. Sometimes I think that the only thing sheep do with any consistency is die. Would you like to see them?" Clegg was proud of his little flock, and although they were of mixed breeds, they looked well, and his lamb crop was not as bad as he sometimes made out.

Josh's eyes brightened. "Delighted!" he said. "I never miss a chance to see someone else's farming."

They walked down to the sheep field and Josh looked them over with an approving nod. "They look well," he commented. "Quite a few twins for this time of year. I see you're using a Dartmoor tup. Ever thought of using a Suffolk on your ewes?"

Clegg shook his head.

"Well, I'm going to this autumn. Tell you what. I've got four young Suffolk rams at home, and I may not be needing all of them - depends on my shepherd. I'll lend you one to try on a score of your ewes and you can compare him with your old tup. What do you say?"

Clegg shrugged. "What can I say? It's a generous offer. Thank you very much."

"Good. That's settled, then. I like to see a chap take an interest in his stock, and you've worked hard at it. I've watched you." He laughed. "Not much escapes the locals, you know, and hard work puts a man high in their estimation."

Clegg raised his eyebrows. "I thought they considered me an outsider."

"So they do, so they do. You'll not be a local for at least twenty years, but that doesn't mean you've got to shut yourself off. You may be from upcountry, but if you meet us halfway, you'll find we're not such a bad lot." He smiled.

"You ask old Tacky. He's been telling everybody in the King's Head what a good chap you are." They both laughed and moved on to where the cattle were grazing. "Nice bunch. You've got an eye for a good beast. Are they pure-bred?"

Clegg shook his head. "I've always thought that pedigree breeding was a rich man's game."

"Don't you believe it!" Josh exclaimed. "It takes as much to feed a poor beast as a good one, and there's always a little bit extra to be had from selling the bulls. You might do well with a small but high-quality herd. Think about it, and if you decide to go pedigree, let me know. I've got a nice little heifer that we've had to separate from the bunch because she's getting bullied. You can have her at normal store price. How's that?"

Clegg laughed. "You'd make a damned good salesman. I'll have to think about it when I see how the lamb crop sells."

They returned to the yard, and Josh climbed into the Land Rover and pressed the starter button. "Right. So, it will be the first Thursday in March at the King's Head. See you then."

Clegg nodded and watched Josh drive slowly up the track and out of the road gate, then he turned to lean on the gate and gaze at his flock. Yes, they were not a bad lot. He would try the Suffolk and perhaps plump for only one breed of ewe to get uniformity, and it might be more profitable to have pure-bred cattle. He might even do some showing. He thought of rosettes and silver cups and name in the local paper. He shut his eyes, but the dream was empty, for Cathy was not there.

March brought a drying wind from the north-east that rattled the hazels and set the elms moaning. Cloud shadows moved swiftly across the moor, and the yellow bent grass sighed as the wind combed out its dead leaves and sent them spinning before it. Rivulets shrank back to their courses, gullies dried, and the Asher resumed its tranquillity.

At night, the grey fox hunted from Cragg Tor to Trenden, from Barton Coppice to the Ashton road. During the day, he lay wherever daylight found him, seeking dark, dry places to curl and sleep. This was his territory, encompassing all that was Ravenscoombe, and around which he set an invisible barrier by scenting trees and stones with the pungent excretion from the glands at the root of his tail. By this, he proclaimed the coombe his, and any outside fox intruded at its peril.

He haunted the Ravenscoombe farmyard and set Skipper barking. Clegg heard him clatter the dustbins, but the fox took no more lambs, for the warmer, longer days had quickened nature's pulse. Voles and young rabbits were abundant, while frogs, worms and beetles made a varied diet on which a fox could grow fat.

CHAPTER 12

THE FIRST THURSDAY in March dawned with a fine drizzle that cleared before Josh and Tom drew out the hounds for the day's hunting. The season had been hard and flesh difficult to come by so that many of the older ones looked ribby and worn. Josh selected a mixed pack of dogs and bitches from the younger 'entry' but also drew out four and a half couple of experienced hounds, including Warrior, Victress and Melody, to steady the pack. Sixteen and a half couple stood expectantly in the yard while the remainder howled mournfully, knowing they were to be left behind.

At ten o'clock, the ancient horsebox was started after a flat battery had been exchanged with one from the blue tractor, and with George Slade to give an extra hand, the hounds were boxed in the front compartment. Jenny then led the two hunt horses, Grizelda and the chestnut, up the ramp behind them and made a last-minute check of saddles, rugs and bandages. Finally, Tom put the two scarlet coats into the cab and they were ready for off.

Clegg finished his morning chores and unloaded the last bag of meal from the back of the ex-Army jeep that served him as a maid of all work. He dusted the bonnet where the white insignia of the United States still showed, and tying Skipper in the back seat, set off for the King's Head and his first encounter with the fox-hunting fraternity en masse.

The meet was at eleven o'clock and when Clegg drew up at a quarter to, there were already a number of mounted and foot followers standing in the pub yard, and space was at a premium among the cars, trailers and horseboxes in the car park. The bar was open, and Tacky's bicycle leaning against the wall indicated that he was at his usual place inside.

Clegg stood apart and surveyed the scene. He was surprised at the small number of riders. He had expected a hoard of red-coated gentlemen in top hats but could see only one. All the rest were in black or very ordinary looking tweed jackets. The foot followers seemed to be mostly farmers or farm workers with a smattering of tweedy women in wellington boots.

They stood around in little groups with Jack Russell terriers straining against unaccustomed leashes while their owners talked about hunting, and the price of hay, and how the winter wheat had suffered in the floods.

There was a murmur of "Here they are," as the battered horsebox drew into a lay-by a hundred yards from the inn. Josh had no desire to unload his precious hounds in the middle of a whole lot of yapping dogs and uncertain horses. Grizelda and the chestnut were led out and helping hands whipped off rugs and removed the protective bandages from legs and tails. Josh and Tom removed their working jackets and donned the scarlet to add a sudden splash of colour to the scene. Then Tom opened the side door of the box and the pack tumbled out. White, ochre, brown, black, they milled round the Master's legs while he called them by name and rewarded his favourites with a morsel of biscuit. Every now and then, a hound would throw back its head and croon.

"That's my beauties!" Josh called in delight. "Sing away, then!" He moved over to Grizelda and swung into the saddle, while the pack crowded round, touching her legs, walking beneath her belly, but she moved not a muscle. There would be no bucking this morning.

"Hounds, please, gentlemen!" Hats were doffed in a ritual long extinct in everyday life, as the Master led his hounds into the pub yard. The landlord handed generous glasses of whisky to the Master and whipper-in, while sloe gin and well-watered Scotch was offered to every rider who looked old enough to drink. Glass in one hand, reins and whip in the other, Tom disciplined the pack with his rating growl, "Ranter, leave it! Tipster, what are you doing?" so that none of the thirty-three hounds strayed more than a yard or two from the Master's horse.

Josh eyed the mounted field and was relieved to see no more than twenty riders: about average for a weekday. Most he recognised as farmers or farmers' wives in black coats and hunting caps. Briggs was out in scarlet and a topper, the only man in the hunt to wear one, and his wife was resplendent in a dark blue coat and hunting cap to match. Both, Josh noticed, were immaculately turned out on expensive-looking 'blood' horses. There was a smattering of the pony club, most of whom were playing truant from school, and Josh smiled as he thought of the number of colds, sore throats and other excuses he had used on hunting days. Secure behind his canine barrier, Josh felt happily insulated from the crowd and its idle chatter. Then he saw Clegg and nudged the mare towards him.

"Glad you could come," he said. Clegg found himself surrounded by hounds and the object of a good deal of curiosity from the bystanders.

"We shall be drawing your land this afternoon," Josh continued in a voice just loud enough for those nearby to hear.

Clegg realised he had been made part of the proceedings and was not sure whether he liked the idea or not. The few words had an almost instant effect. A large red-faced man immediately struck up a conversation, saying that you couldn't be too careful nowadays with so many 'anti' people about. Clegg could only think of saying "No, you couldn't," in a rather lame voice.

He was saved from further words from the large man by a loud voice behind him saying, "I'm Briggs, I believe we're neighbours."

Clegg looked up at the man in the scarlet coat and took the offered hand with a nod.

"Been meaning to get in touch with you," Briggs continued, trying to control his restive mount. "Water Authority's been asking to survey part of my ground that borders yours. Didn't say what for, but I thought I'd better tell you. They're tricky beggars. Never know what they're up to. Well, it looks as though we're off."

He glanced across at Josh who was looking at his watch. The Master took the copper horn from between the first two buttons of his coat and blew a single note. "Hounds, please! Hounds, please!" A swathe cleared in front of the pack as the cavalcade moved off towards the Barton.

The Master and whip had worked out a rough plan of action the night before, and providing the wind stayed in the same quarter, they would draw upwind from Barton Plantation, through the water meadows by way of the oak coppice and on to Colspit where Josh hoped to find the grey fox. Tacky had been instructed to stop up all the earths he knew in the coombe, and this the old man had done.

Josh stopped by the rails that barred the way into the plantation and waved his hounds into the covert. Eagerly, they disappeared among the spruce trees while the Master stood listening, waiting for the whimper that would tell of a fox. Tom had galloped to the far end of the wood to keep lookout, leaving the rest of the riders grouped a few yards behind Josh. In a loud voice, Mrs Briggs was telling someone which way the fox was going to go, and Josh chuckled to himself, for he didn't know and neither did the hounds, so how the hell did she?

A youth cantered up, red-faced and conscious of being late, his grey Arab pony spattered with mud and sweat. He wore an old brown jacket torn at the sleeve, and boots that were a size too large, but he sat on the little horse as though it grew out from under him.

Josh again heard the voice of Mrs Briggs expressing the opinion that such scruffiness should not be tolerated, and that in her day he would have been sent home. The boy flushed and moved away to stand alone, his gaze on the wood.

Josh beckoned him over. "What's your name, son?"

The boy bit his lip and looked anxiously in the direction of the indignant Mrs Briggs. "Robert Petherick, sir."

"Any relation to Bill Petherick?"

The boy nodded. "My father."

Josh smiled. "Ah! Well then, Robert, would you do something for me? Would you ride to the other side of this wood and keep an eye out? If you see a fox, don't holler, just come quietly back and tell me." He leant down with a confidential wink. "We'll keep it to ourselves for a little while." The boy grinned and, setting his heels to the pony, jumped the rails and cantered off up the ride.

Josh looked back at Mrs Briggs who, for once, was silent. When you can ride like that, he thought, you'll have something to talk about. He gathered his reins. "Would you please stay here?" he called back as he put Grizelda at the rails and jumped into the wood.

Inside it was quiet save for the rustle of hounds working through the undergrowth, and Josh thought how fine it would be not to have the 'field' to contend with. But it was their subscriptions that paid the bills, or at least most of them. If only he could find that thousand a year, just for a few more years.

A jay squawked, and somewhere over the other side a flock of rooks were set cawing. The grey pony and its rider appeared round a bend in the ride. "There's one gone out down the bottom, Huccaby!" Robert gasped.

"Well done, lad. What sort was he?"

The boy wheeled the pony. "Oh, a girt sandy coloured 'un. He went towards Ashton Bridge."

"Right, Robert, we'll lay 'em on before we let the others know, eh?" Josh trotted towards the far side of the wood, blowing his horn to bring the distant hounds to him. "Now, show me where he came out," he said as they pushed out of the trees into a grass field.

"Down by that fallen tree, sir. He went over the field and through that gate." The boy pointed.

Josh stood in his stirrups. "Come up! Come up! Lieu on, my beauties! Whoop, Melody! Whoop, Warrior!"

He blew a series of sharp urgent notes on the horn and cantered the pack towards the gateway. There, Warrior found the line and spoke with a deep ominous howl. Melody took it up, then Rampton and Rufus.

Tom appeared from nowhere to call out the rest of the pack, counting them as they emerged from the wood. "All on, sir!" he called as the pack clamoured into full cry and the first of the riders appeared out of the wood.

"Well done, Tom!" Josh shouted. "We've got 'em. Away sharp. Better get on down to the river. He'll likely turn there. Young Petherick here will be my second whip." He grinned at the boy. "You stick close to me, lad." They galloped stride for stride, the big roan hunter pounding head down, while the grey striding alongside seemed hardly to touch the ground. Josh let

Grizelda take her own course down the big grass field, while he kept his eyes on the leading hounds, Melody, Victress and Warrior. In front loomed a big hedge bank which he knew was not wired. "Follow me if you can!" he called to the youth as he turned towards a place where the haw thorn thinned. He steadied the mare, pointed her head at the bank and dug his heels in. She took two strides, and with a grunt, landed on top, paused for a second, then dropped on the other side. Josh glanced back but the grey was already alongside, its rider sitting easily, his eyes bright with excitement. There was a crash behind as a horse fell. Hard luck, Josh thought as he pushed the roan down a steep incline towards the river where Tom was waving him to turn right.

At the riverbank, the hounds checked and began to cast up and down. Josh pulled the horn from his jacket and blew once. Every head went up and he 'lifted' them in the direction Tom had indicated.

"He ran up stream just in the water!" the whip called. "I lost sight of him by the willows!"

"Come along! Come along! Try up! Try up!" The Master encouraged the pack towards the willow clump. Suddenly, Warrior spoke, then stood and bayed by a fallen tree trunk, and Josh pulled up his sweating mare. "Damn, he's gone to earth in an old otter hole. Where the hell's the terrier?"

At that moment, a familiar sweat-stained trilby bobbed along the Ashton Bridge and a few seconds later, Tacky Bowden hobbled along the riverbank, carrying Tiger in his arms as though he were the most valuable dog ever whelped. "Yer us be, Master," he puffed, and then in a more confidential tone asked, "Be 'er the grey 'un, Josh?"

Josh shook his head. "No, a big sandy coloured fox. But let's try that dog of yours."

Tacky placed himself and Tiger by the tree roots while Tom dismounted and poked about inside the hole with his crop. "He's in there," he said, "and there's another opening just up there."

He pointed to a hole a little way upstream, and Josh turned the mare and called the pack away. "Right, we'll try and bolt him. Here, my beauties! Come along. Leave it!" He took them twenty yards into the field where they sat in a tight bunch, watching the men by the river and waiting for the whoop that would release them from the Master's control.

Josh nodded and Tacky put the terrier down the hole. The dog went in without hesitation, the hackles bristling on his tawny back, while his master knelt down to put his ear to the ground. "I can 'ear 'un," he said quietly.

The field had stopped chattering and stood in a bunch behind the pack. Every now and then, a hound would creep forward to be rated by Josh's raucous "Git back there!" Suddenly Tom gave a yell and the pack cascaded down the hill as the fox darted out and ran up the field towards the riders. The hounds were too slow to turn as he bolted between the horses' legs while the men "yoi-ed" and "Taiyouw-ed". A girl in pigtails was bucked off, to mount again immediately, flushed and mud-stained. Horses wheeled and snorted as the pack followed the fox, and Josh cursed people, horses, everything, for getting in the way.

It was Warrior who sorted out the line from the maze of horses and man scents. His belling tongue called them on as he squeezed between the bars of a gate and into the plough. The gate was padlocked.

"Ah well," thought Josh, "there's nothing for it." He shortened his reins and pushed Grizelda on with a loud "Gorr-on!" She rattled the top bar but recovered her balance and landed safely on the other side. "That'll sort a few of 'em out," he thought, then looked down to see the grey Arab's nose come level with his knee, while its rider stood in his stirrups to ease the weight on the pony's loins.

Tom appeared from nowhere and the three of them galloped up a dead furrow ten yards behind the tail hounds. On the far side of the plough, a tall hedge and ditch barred the way. The sandy fox made a desperate leap, fell back into the ditch and spun round to bite deep into Melody's neck. The hound yelped with pain, but the loosed folds of skin protected her from serious harm and she shook the fox free as Victress' teeth crunched through its backbone, and it knew no more.

By the time Josh arrived, Tarquin and Ranter were fighting over a leg while the rest of the pack, spattered with blood, clawed and pulled at the remainder. The Master dismounted and ran eagerly into the melee, whooping and encouraging his hounds to "Eat him up, my beauties!" For this was their reward, this was what their instinct and centuries of breeding commanded them to do.

Josh retrieved the carcass, cut the brush and peeled it from the bone, then he walked over to where the boy stood with his back to the hounds while his pony cropped the grass that bordered the ditch. "Would you like the brush?" Josh asked. There was no reply and Josh repeated a little louder, "Would you like the brush? You deserve it."

The boy turned slowly. Gone was the flush of excitement. Instead, the face was pale and drawn. "Thank you," he said quietly. "Father'll be pleased." He paused and looked uncertain for a moment as the Master wiped the blood from his hands. "I suppose we had to kill it," he said.

Josh frowned and shook his head as though the question were irrelevant. He pulled himself up on to the mare. "That's what it's all about, Robert," was all he could think of saying.

At that moment, the rest of the 'field' arrived, breathless and sweating. "Oh, damn!" Mrs Briggs whined in a loud voice. "We've missed the kill, and I was looking forward to getting the brush." She looked at Josh, but he avoided her gaze.

The youth held out the sandy remnant. "You can have it if you want it," he said.

Mrs Briggs' eyes widened. "'S'trordinary boy!" she said.

The Master blew his horn and they moved on to draw through the oak coppice, then across the water meadows to the edge of Colspit. Here, he paused to confer with his whipper-in. "Tricky place this, Tom, with that big old quarry. We don't want any more hounds with busted ribs. You'd better go on to the bottom by the mill ruin and I'll post someone at point above the quarry." He beckoned to the youth. "You still game, lad?"

The boy nodded.

"Good, now go along the top of this wood to that corner." He pointed with his whip. "If you see one go away, give a holler." He watched the grey go and pondered the rider's eagerness to hunt and his distaste for the kill. He shrugged. Perhaps that was how he had been as a boy. He couldn't remember.

It began to drizzle. Good, Josh thought. It will improve the scent and make most of the 'field' head for home. He looked behind and sure enough Mrs Briggs had left her husband's side and was riding in the direction of The Barton, while several more were saying good night with hats raised. Eventually, half a dozen horsemen remained to sit hunched against the rain.

When he judged that Tom was in position, Josh urged Grizelda over the low bank to take his hounds into the wood. "Try up! Try up! Lieu! Lieu!" He called his encouragement as they padded over the soft leaf mould and pushed through the undergrowth, noses to the ground and sterns waving. Pigeons clattered out, a grey squirrel scurried down one elm and up another. Dancer whimpered and babbled over a rabbit run and was rated with a gutteral "Ware riot! Leave it, Dancer! Leave it!" Slowly, silently, the rest of the pack worked up the wood in search of the one pungent scent that would set them screaming. Tarquin found a scenting post and growled his hatred, but the signs were stale and there was no flight line to cause him to give tongue. He cocked his leg against it and moved on.

Bashful caught a claw in some barbed wire and yelped once, but Josh knew it was pain, not anger, that caused it. Then Warrior's great voice boomed out, and every hound stopped, head up, listening. Again, the old hound's cry echoed through the wood, a cry thick with hatred and blood lust, for he knew the scent.

"Get on to Warrior!" Good ol' dog! Get on to him, my beauties!" Josh urged the pack to where the tan hound ran. He spurred Grizelda through the tangle of branches, at the same time doubling urgent notes on the horn as first Ranter and then Tarquin took up the cry. As they pushed out of the wood, he heard a shrill voice from the corner of the wood and saw the boy waving his hat in the air, cantering towards Trenden Wood. Josh caught him up at some sheep hurdles. "Wait for 'em, boy," he panted. "Did you see him?"

"Yes, sir, a grey 'un he was. Went through that gap."

Josh gave the mare a kick. "That's the one, boy, that's the one!" he shouted as she jumped the hurdles. "Come on. They're all on."

The pack clamoured in a long line after the tan hound. Josh stood in his stirrups to get a better view over the next field and saw a pair of jays fly squawking and scolding from the edge of Trenden Wood. At the same time, Warrior scrambled up the bank and disappeared into the undergrowth. "He's gone into Trenden!" Josh called and indicated to Tom that he should get around the other side of the wood.

Inside Trenden, the clamour resounded among the tall conifers and Josh pulled up the mare until he could judge in which direction the sound was going. "He's on through," he said to the youth. "Come on. He'll give us a run yet!"

They galloped up the deep rutted track where spruce pit props were stacked in neat piles awaiting collection, then they turned into the old woodland where oak and ash had smothered the undergrowth so that the hounds could be seen weaving between the great trunks.

Suddenly, there was silence, and Josh reined in the mare and listened. "Damn! They've lost him," he growled.

"Taiyouw! Away!" Tom's voice came from the far side of the wood, and Josh doubled on his horn and they were away again. At the wood's edge, Melody picked up the line and by the time the riders had found a gate, Josh gave Grizelda a breather until he saw which way the pack went when it reached the fence at the bottom, and as they scrambled straight through he muttered, "He's on for the moor," and sent the mare off after them. They found a gate and were on grass again. Josh held his hand up and stopped as the leading hounds wavered and began casting backwards and forwards.

"Anybody see him?" he asked, glancing back. No one had. He scanned the moor beyond the next stone wall and thought he saw a grey shape dart between two clumps of gorse. He looked towards the skyline in the direction the fox was going, and black against the darkening sky stood the stones of Hods Barrow.

Once more, Warrior spoke to the line and, more slowly now, the pack hunted down to the wall and scrambled over. Josh cantered down the slope with a feeling of foreboding he could not explain. He steadied the mare, and three strides from the wall, dug his heels in her flanks. She took one more stride and took off, and in that second Josh knew she would hit it. He heard her front shoes rap the stones and felt her tip forward. There came a sickening thud and a great weight across his loins, then nothing more.

The leading riders watched horrified as the roan somersaulted over the wall. They saw her land on the far side and lie still with the Master beneath her.

Tom dismounted and climbed over the wall as the mare struggled to get up. She was only winded, but her rider did not move. Briggs turned his thoroughbred and spurred it back towards the road and the line of cars, one of which was dispatched for a doctor. Then the scarlet-coated figure was galloping back and in a few seconds was over the wall and kneeling beside Josh.

"Don't move him. Loosen his stock. Slade, you'd better get after the hounds." The orders rapped out, and Briggs was once more Major Briggs and in command.

As the whip turned to go, Josh opened his eyes. "God, what's happened?" he asked weakly, then as his brain cleared. "Oh yes, that bloody wall. How's the mare?"

"All right," Briggs assured him. "How do you feel?"

"Same," Josh replied. "Can't feel a thing." He closed his eyes as though the light hurt. "Damned grey fox," he muttered. "They always spell trouble ... " His words faded into inaudibility.

"He's only half-conscious," whispered Briggs. "Rambling a bit."

Suddenly Josh struggled to get up. "Tom! Tom! Are you there?"

"Yes, boss."

"Tom, did you see him? There was a grey fox, wasn't there?" Josh's voice was a hoarse whisper. "He's gone to Hods Barrow, Tom ... Hods Barrow. Better watch he doesn't ... " He closed his eyes again and sank into oblivion.

CHAPTER 13

THE GREY FOX breasted the mound where the rough granite stones lay in broad rings and paused to look back. The line of hounds laboured up the slope, now hesitating, then bunching, and again streaming on, giving vent to their rage. He ran his tongue round his jowl and tested the wind before turning to stretch his long legs at a fast run down a heather-covered gully. At the bottom of the slope, the gully still held water and he pattered down it to a small stream, then, still in the water, ran on towards Stannon Marsh.

The pack followed steadily to the top of the gully, but where the vegetation closed over they faltered and spread out, hunting backwards and forwards through the brown heather until all but one threw up its head and trotted back to the whip's call. Warrior, however, hunted on. The faint scent in the gully was not enough to make him cry out, but it was sufficient to keep him working steadily downhill. At the stream, he crossed and re-crossed the stones until a single wet pad mark put him on the line. Now he trotted, testing every rock, every dry stone, for the scent of his quarry.

He reached the marsh and cried once where the fox had trodden the short turf. The sound was heard by Tom as he and the boy gathered the pack, and for a moment they paused to listen, then the whip blew hard on the horn to recall the hound, but the tan shape hunted on. Tom turned wearily and called the rest of the pack to leave it. One by one, they gathered round the chestnut's heels and as wraiths of mist drifted through the stones of Hods Barrow, the two riders led the hounds slowly back to the knot of horsemen and the one prostrate figure in a scarlet coat.

Warrior did not hear the horn, for his brain was single-purposed and the taint of the grey fox still clung to the wet tussocks. A dense greyness closed in to swirl about him as he ran, head down, along the sheep tracks. But neither hunter or hunted needed eyes; their noses and ears told them all they had to know: the one to find the way, the other to follow.

The fox quit the shelter of a thorn tree when he heard the grating alarm note of a snipe as it zigzagged between the reed clumps. He loped on towards Cragg Tor as his ears caught the sound of heavy paws splashing through water. Among the rocks below the tor, Warrior gave tongue, a single harsh wail that caused the fox to turn away from the shallow earth on Cragg Tor and run on towards the open moor. Past Fist Rock and out of the mist into the clear night over Ashton Down, where the spongy turf spattered to the quadruple rhythm of the fox's pads, and a few seconds later to the heavier tread of the hound.

Under the waning moor they ran, from Ashton Cleave to Sheepworthy where Farmer Wonnacott saw them by the light of his tractor headlamps as they crossed the road to Kit Spinney. The fox ran to the edge of the main wood that halves the moor and padded along the tarmac until a stream of light and noise turned him and he left the stench of machines to confuse his long pursuer. Warrior dodged the car's headlamps while the driver swerved and cursed, and then wondered if he had seen aright. The old hound worked along the verge until he found the line once more and howled his vengeance to the fox.

Out of his own territory, the fox sought the tracks and animal paths that made running easier, all the while following the unconscious instinct that drew him round in a circle and back towards Ravenscoombe.

And so it was that Clegg saw them as he made the last rounds of his sheep. At first he thought the shape loping towards him was a dog, for it made no effort to avoid him. He knew it must have seen him, for the moonlight was bright, and not until it stopped ten paces away did he see that it was the grey fox.

The latter stared at him with glazed eyes, but saw only a blurred outline, for his senses were dulled with fatigue and his muscles functioned automatically so that he ran without knowing towards the one refuge he could remember: the old badger sett in Colspit Wood.

The night breeze wafted the man scent towards him and he curled back his lips to show the long white canine teeth. Then he turned to go, but the exhausted muscles had stiffened in the few moments of inactivity and he could hardly walk as the second shape emerged from the shadows. The footsore hound limped into the moonlight, his nose still to the ground, and Clegg watched the two animals draw closer, the fox staggering at a snail's pace down the hill and the hound unaware of anything outside the faint scent of his enemy and the need to keep moving, and while the watcher recognised his old adversary the grey fox, and wanted him dead, he could not stand by and see the final drama enacted.

"Warrior, come here!" Clegg's word of command made the hound hesitate for a moment, and he stopped, nose poised an inch above the ground, then snorted and hunted on. Clegg called louder, this time trying to put the rough edge into his voice that he had heard Josh use when disciplining the pack. "Warrior! Leave it!" The hound raised his head, and the thread was broken.

Warrior limped over to the familiar figure and Clegg held him by the scruff as he watched the fox jerk painfully across the stones by the stream.

He paused to look back, then a cloud passed over the moon and Clegg saw him no more.

Warrior was put back into the loft with food and water. Clegg decided to return him in the morning when he could tell Josh what he had seen. He went into the kitchen and lit the lamp. "Yes, it makes quite a yarn," he said out loud as he sat down and took writing paper from the table drawer. He wrote a letter to Cathy as he had done most weeks since she left. A normal letter, no histrionics, just telling her how he was getting on. He had ceased to ask her to return to Ravenscoombe. Then instead of his usual little note to Stephen, he took a fresh piece of paper and headed it "THE SAGA OF THE GREY FOX". Underneath, he began to write.

He told how the fox had come to the coombe, how Warrior had been injured and the Master had left him in the loft. He listed the fox's exploits, the lambs and chickens he had taken, and described how he had fallen through the roof. The story of the Ackland Fox was retold, and how Huccaby's father had bought the same horse twice. He set down a sober version of the escapade with the one-eyed cat, and described the meet at the King's Head, finally telling of the encounter with the hunted and the hunter by the stream in Ravenscoombe and how he had stopped Warrior from catching the fox.

When it was done, Clegg sat back with a sigh of pleasure. Then he wrote on the bottom in large capitals "TO BE CONTINUED".

"There", he said, "that should interest him. Perhaps he'll write." He addressed the fat envelope to his father-in-law's house, frowning as he realised that he did not even know if they were still staying there. They could have moved, he supposed, but surely Cathy would leave a forwarding address. They must be all right, otherwise he would have heard. After all, they were still officially married. He resolved that, as soon as lambing was over, he would ask Tacky to keep an eye on the place and he would go to Southampton to sort things out.

The next morning, Clegg loaded Warrior into the back of the jeep and drove to Menaridden. Uncertain where to go, he went to the back of the house and knocked on the kitchen door. Mabel Slade answered, red-eyed and with her hair still loose about her shoulders. She looked at Clegg and shook her head. "'Tis a turrible thing," she said before he could open his mouth.

"What is?" Clegg asked.

"Why, 'uccaby a-lyin' there in th' hospital." She brushed back her hair with one hand. "I'm afeared us be in a right pickle this mornin'."

Clegg still looked mystified. "I'm sorry, but could you tell me what's happened?" he asked.

"Don' 'ee know then? Why, 'ee've 'urt 'is back 'untin'. Serious they do say. 'Co'rse they won't tell us nothin' but us reckons as 'ee've broken 'un." She fished in her apron for a handkerchief and blew her nose loudly. "Now what can us do fer 'ee then, zur?" Her practised eye had noted the collar and tie and together with his upcountry accent, she judged the visitor warranted the "Zur".

Clegg told her about Warrior and she directed him to the kennels. It was not until he turned to go that the full implication of what she had been saying dawned.

An air of gloom pervaded the kennels as Clegg drew up. Even the hounds appeared listless as they walked round their exercise yards while Tom and his father hosed down the flagstones.

The whip walked over when he spotted Warrior. "Ah, I see you've got him then," he said in a flat tone of voice. "We wondered where he'd got to."

Clegg was going to tell them about the events of the night before, but now it seemed pointless and out of place. "I've just heard the news," he said. "How did it happen?"

Tom shrugged. "They hit the top of a wall when we were on to that damned grey fox. The mare turned over and the boss was underneath. He was hurt pretty bad. Missus has been with him all night." He untied Warrior and led him away. "He's knocked himself up," he commented as the hound walked stiff-legged across the yard. "I wonder if he killed that fox?"

"No, he didn't. I saw it," Clegg replied without embellishing the tale.

"More's the pity," Tom said and slammed the yard gate. "Thanks for bringing him back anyway."

On the way home, Clegg called at Tacky's cottage to give him the news. "Us were there when it 'appened," the old man told him. "Leastways us weren't far away. 'Tis a bad business, but 'er 'ave allus bin one fer takin' risks when they 'ounds are a-runnin'. Owzum, us'll do no good crackin' on in the doorway. Come in an' 'ave a cup o' tea."

They sat down while Clegg told the old man what he had seen the night before. Tacky gave one of his long-drawn-out "Ahhh"s as he poured the tea.

"'Er must've 'unted that ol' beggar fer nigh four hours," he said. "Us'll 'ave t' get 'un, Clegg. 'Ee's a grey 'un, an' they'm allus unlucky. Us'll get no peace until 'er's ketched."

"It's just a fox," Clegg reassured him. "Surely you don't believe in this fairy story about grey foxes?"

Tacky shook his head. "I told 'ee afore, this 'un's no ordinary fox, 'er's crafty an' 'er's grey, an' whether us believes in the Ackland fox or no, this 'un's turning out to be a master at bringin' bad luck."

Clegg sipped the dark brew and smiled indulgently at the old man's foibles.

He was still musing over Tacky's superstition when he arrived back at Ravenscoombe. As he opened the back door, he saw that two letters were propped on the window sill. The official-looking one he ignored in his eagerness to open the second, for it was addressed in Cathy's handwriting, although the postmark was Boston, U.S.A. The slightly scented notepaper stirred memories he thought he had forgotten, and emotions he imagined he could do without. Now he knew he had been wrong. He tore open the envelope and scanned the letter with a pang of disappointment as he saw how painfully short it was. He sat down and read:

Dear Clegg,

I find it difficult to write after not hearing from you for such a long while. When I left, I said you would have to choose between the farm and me. I meant it, Clegg, and I assume your silence means that you have made your choice. I could not bury myself again, without friends, miles from anywhere.

It is possible that Stephen feels differently, but he is a boy and can make his own choice when he is old enough. In the meantime, Daddy has agreed to pay for his schooling provided we do not return to Devon, or alternatively that you give up the farm and go back to your old job.

Stephen and I have been touring the States and Canada on a sort of fact-finding tour for the plastics factory. Daddy arranged it all and he has all the forwarding addresses, so there was no excuse for not writing. I'm sorry it has turned out this way, Clegg, but if you had only written. Stephen sends his love.

Yours,
Cathy.

Clegg felt a dryness in his throat as he read and re-read the letter. "But I did write," he said vehemently. "I wrote nearly every week." He thought for a moment, then clenched his fist so that the letter crumpled. "Bloody father-in-law! He's been hanging on to them!" He smoothed the sheet of paper, folded it carefully and put it in his inside pocket. Then he ran out of the house and with a grind, headed the jeep for Ashton.

At the post office, he drafted a simple message: "LETTERS SENT SOUTHAMPTON. COME HOME. CLEGG." He read it through, added the words "I LOVE YOU", and sent it to the hotel in Boston. Then he made a telephone call to the plastics factory and Cathy's father. The voice at the other end was biting and cool.

"I considered it my duty as a father ... dragging my daughter into that insanitary hovel ... She won't be back until August at the earliest ... I intend to suggest she starts divorce proceedings."

Clegg fumed. "You bloody well send those letters on!" he roared and slammed the receiver down. What was the use of arguing further? The damage was done.

On the way home, he pulled in at the King's Head. It was lunchtime and the regulars, including Tacky, were playing dominoes in the public bar. Clegg ordered a whisky and Tacky left his game to join him in the corner. Why, me 'anzum, you look proper crabby. Where 'ave 'ee been to that's got 'ee so worked up? Tidn't cos ol' Josh fer certain."

Clegg pulled at his beard and said nothing, draining his glass in two gulps.

Tacky picked it up. "I'll get the next," he said. "Same?"

Clegg shook his head, "No, I'll have a beer, thank you."

Tacky smiled. "Ah, that's better. Whisky's fer 'ard drinkin'. Beer's fer bein' social."

He fetched two foaming pints and put them on the table. Clegg took a sip and wiped the froth from his moustache. "Cheers!" He sat back with a sigh. "I've just had a flaming row with my father-in-law. He's been holding on to some letters that should have been sent to my wife."

"Oh arr," Tacky nodded, "an' 'oo is this father-in-law as is so 'igh an' mighty?"

Clegg took several quick gulps, "Just because he owns Tidworth Plastics doesn't mean he can rule my life or Cathy's." He raised his glass again.

"Yer, 'old 'ard, me anzum. If you goes on like that, you'll be blowed up afore us gets the next pints in. Tidworth Plastics, eh? An' they'm to Southampton, if I remember what you said th' other night. Well, if you wants t'go an set about 'un proper us'll look to they sheep o' yorn."

"Not much point now," Clegg sighed. "She won't be back until August."

He slumped back into the corner. "What a bloody mess."

The old man thought for a moment, then leant over and tapped Clegg's shoulder, "Don' 'ee worry, 'er'll turn up all right, you'll see. Now let's 'ave that other pint an' a pasty, an' you'll face th' day better."

While they ate, Tacky turned the conversation to the misfortune of others and they agreed to visit Josh in hospital as soon as possible. They played darts until closing time, then Clegg pushed Tacky's bike into the back of the jeep and drove him home.

He pulled into his own yard and sat for a moment or two looking at the house. "I suppose it is a bit primitive," he said to himself, "but with a bit more time and a bit more money ... Ah well, what's the use?"

He backed the jeep under the old cart shed and walked slowly to the back door, pausing to inspect the place where the rain had grouted out the stones of the yard. It was a losing battle.

Inside the porch, he stepped on the official letter which had fallen from its place on the sill. "Another Ministry return," he told himself as he picked it up and walked through to the kitchen. Carelessly, he opened it and began to read, then he sat down at the table and read it again. It too was a short letter, not from the Ministry of Agriculture, but from the Water Authority. It said quite simply that the Ravenscoombe Valley was being considered as one of two sites for a reservoir. They asked permission to survey the land adjacent to Colspit Wood and said that someone would call and discuss the matter with him "at your earliest convenience."

Clegg looked at the piece of paper for several seconds. It was polite, even considerate, but it might just as well have said: "Dear Sir, we wish to drown your farm. Regretfully yours."

"Just like that," he said, throwing the letter on to the table. "They can decide just like that!" He snapped his fingers. "All that back-breaking work, for what?"

Clegg ran his fingers through his thick mop of black hair with a quick motion of despair. Not only was he in danger of losing his wife, he was likely to lose his farm as well. It was no longer a question of either, but both.

CHAPTER 14

JOSH SLOWLY OPENED his eyes and gazed up at the white ceiling. He had begun to know that ceiling very well. There was a hair crack that meandered from above his head to somewhere behind his line of vision beyond the screens. He found himself wondering what a crack was doing in the brand new ceiling of a brand new hospital, and whether he could move just enough to see where it ended. He glanced along his nose at the two humps at the foot of the bed. They were still there, immovable: two alien lumps of flesh and bone that were once his legs.

He turned his head sideways. She was still there, sitting in the chair with her head slumped forward in the half-sleep that comes of worry and fatigue. It seemed to Josh that Isobel had been there ever since the first night when the surgeon's needle had brought oblivion. She was there holding his hand as he slid into unconsciousness; she was still there when he came round the next morning, and all the next day, and the next.

Isobel stirred, and a lock of hair fell across her face. Josh remembered the girl he had taken on honeymoon, the pretty girl whose hair shone in the Italian sun, and who laughed at his antics in the water. He had watched that flower wilt, too wrapped up in his own world to realise it. He sighed. Isobel looked up suddenly and smiled, and it was all there again, the girl and the hair and the sun.

"Feeling better, dear?" she asked, pushing back the stray lock with a characteristic flick.

He nodded. "How long have you been here?" he asked.

"Oh! Only since lunch. You were asleep most of the morning." She smoothed out the bed covers and drew her chair closer. Josh reached out to take her hand, holding it tight until his knuckles whitened and she gave a little wince of pain, then he relaxed and gently stroked her fingers.

He closed his eyes. "I'm sorry," he said quietly.

"Sorry for what, Josh?"

He did not reply immediately but lay for some time contemplating the ceiling. "Sorry for everything," he said at last. "For not living up to your expectations, for thinking too much about the hounds and the farm and myself, mostly myself." He turned to look at her. "Three weeks on your back not being able to move, the only thing you can do is think, and I've done a lot of that. He turned back to contemplate the ceiling. "But there's still time, Isobel, there's still time. You'll see, when I get over this - and I will - I'll try and make it up to you."

Isobel straightened his pillows. "I know you will, dear, but in the meantime, we've got to get you well."

Josh took her hand again and this time squeezed it gently. "You're a good sort," he said huskily.

Isobel Huccaby smiled. It was the nearest he would ever get to saying "I love you", and she would have to be content with it.

A nurse came in with a trolley of bottles and stainless steel dishes. "Pill round," she said cheerily, "and you've got some more visitors." She waited while Josh swallowed two large tablets, then pushed her chinking load out of the little ward and into the corridor. A second later, Tacky stood in the doorway resplendent in his best brown suit and highly polished black boots.

Josh's face lit up. "Come in, come in, Thomas Ackland. Don't tell me you've cycled all the way from Ashton?"

Tacky grinned and shook his head. As he stepped inside the room, a tall, dark-haired young man followed and stood behind him. The young man was also grinning as he stroked his chin tentatively, as though feeling for something that was no longer there.

"Good Lord, it's young Clegg," Josh exclaimed. "A bit soon for shearing time, isn't it?" They laughed.

"Well, since I was coming to the big city, I thought I'd better look a bit less like a wild man."

Josh waved his hand, "Isobel, my dear, you know Bowden who used to have Ravenscoombe, and this is Clegg Granger, who has the farm now."

They shook hands as Isobel said, "Oh, yes, we were talking about you the other day. Aren't they thinking of putting a reservoir there or something?"

"What!" Josh exploded. "Nobody told me anything about it. They can't do that, they mustn't! It would be a hell of a nuisance for the hunt to go round that, and in any case," he added as an afterthought, "Clegg here will lose his farm."

"Well, I'm afraid there's nothing you can do about it in here," Isobel said, smoothing his pillows yet again, "and in any case, the cause has been taken up by a Mrs Wrightson who appears to be avidly against it."

"Ar, 'er would be." Tacky grinned at Josh who scowled at the sheets until Isobel folded them down more comfortably.

The nurse put her head round the door. "Only two at a time, please."

Isobel got up. "I'll slip out and do some shopping," she said, kissing Josh on the cheek. "Is there anything you need?"

"Yes, you'd better get me some writing things," Josh grunted. "We can't leave it all to that silly woman."

When Isobel had gone, Tacky took a brown paper bag from his pocket and placed it in the locker beside the bed. The bag stood upright and was bottle shaped.

"There are some paper cups over there," Josh whispered. "Prop my head up and let's have a snort. It'll probably chivvy the old pills round a bit, but here's to you both and thanks for this bit of comfort." They sipped the whisky with many anxious glances towards the door.

"Now, what are we going to do about this reservoir business?" Josh asked.

Clegg shrugged and shook his head. "What can anyone do?" he asked. "There's a choice of two sites, and you can bet with my luck they'll plumb for mine."

"That's defeatist talk," Josh said. "Isn't that so, Tacky?"

The old man nodded.

"No, we'll have to find out a few things first, and I'm surprised at you, Clegg, for not showing a bit more fight."

Tacky looked at the MFH hard and, with a warning gesture, changed the subject. "'Ave 'er told you about seein' th' ol' grey fox?"

Josh shook his head, and Clegg recounted how he had seen the fox and Warrior on the evening of the fateful hunt.

"You shouldn't have stopped the old dog, Clegg," Josh commented. "He would have got him for sure if you had left him alone. Still, it's done now. Tom told me that old Wonnacott saw them below Kit Spinney. They must have run twenty miles from Colspit and back again." He rested his head deep into the pillows. "Just think of it. That old hound sticking to one line for twenty miles of that sort of country. What a run that would have given us! You shouldn't have stopped him. He deserved his taste of that damned grey fox."

Josh went over the events of the fateful hunt until footsteps outside made them hastily screw up the cups and put the bottle into the locker.

Isobel came in and bustled round, straightening things. "Sorry, gentlemen," she said, smiling at Clegg and Tacky. "That's enough for one day. Do come again. You've cheered Josh up no end."

Politely but firmly, she ushered them out into the corridor, and they began to walk to the entrance when Tacky suddenly stopped. "You go on, Clegg," he said. "I've forgotten something," and he turned and went back to the ward.

Clegg waited by the jeep for what seemed an inordinately long time, but eventually Tacky appeared, trotting across the car park. "Sorry," he puffed.

"Just a bit o' business t' clear up." He climbed into the passenger seat where Tiger sat tied with a piece of string. "S'funny," he said as they crawled through the afternoon traffic, "Josh's missus do fuss about 'im like a hen wi' chickens." He chuckled. "I've never seen 'er so broody."

"She seemed a nice person," Clegg said.

"Oh ar!" Tacky nodded. "An' 'er's 'ad a bit to put up with old Josh's not zackly the easiest to 'andle, an' then when 'er lost the lill' maid - "

"Sorry?"

"It were their first baby - didn' ave no more."

"I didn't know that," Clegg said.

"Ar well, 'ee don't know such things till you gets t' know folks. Fair knocked 'em fer six it did wi' 'er in 'ospital an Josh practically livin' wi' they 'ounds of 'is. Would 'ardly step inside th'ouse fer nigh four months."

There was a lull in the conversation while they negotiated the High Street. They drove through the sameness of the suburbs and Clegg thought of the prim little house that had once been home, one of a hundred identical houses each in the same sized rectangle with the same clipped privet and the same tired faces peering over. No, he couldn't go back to that.

Once on the open road again, Tacky relaxed and chatted about his main preoccupation: the catching of the grey fox. "Us'll walk the farm an' put a few more wires down afore the cover gets too thick. Only don't you tell Josh. 'Ee don't sold with 'untin' twixt April an' September." He shook his head. "Six months 'ee chases 'em t'death an' th'other six months 'ee spends makin' sure there's enough t' go round next year. T'idn' no way t' get rid of 'em. They'm only vermin."

Clegg did not reply, hardly hearing what the old man was saying, for his thoughts were far away. Now he knew he wanted Cathy back, but things had become too complicated. Three months ago, it would have been so simple. He could have made his choice and it could have been Cathy. But now the farm might have to go anyway, and if he was forced into selling, would she believe he really wanted her? Or would he end up by losing both? How could he make his point with her three thousand miles away and no way of making contact? He felt as though he were being swept along by circumstances over which he had no control. Fate had taken a hand and was getting it all wrong, and Clegg did not like being manipulated, even by the Almighty.

He clenched his teeth and changed down to pass a lorry, and Tacky clutched the side of the jeep, "Yer, 'old 'ard, me 'anzum. Us'll end up alongside o' Josh if us bain't careful."

"Sorry," Clegg murmured. "I was just thinking about the rotten luck I've been having. One minute things seem more or less tolerable and the next, bang! My wife wants a divorce and the powers that be want to take away my farm."

Tacky shook his head sympathetically. "Now won't you believe that grey foxes brings bad luck?" he said ruefully.

Clegg skidded to a halt at Tacky's gate and watched the old man pick his way between the puddles to his back door. A solitary figure with just a dog for company. Clegg sighed, and one thought bothered him as he drove the jeep into his own yard. When would his own chosen solitude merge into the enforced loneliness that was Tacky's lot.

He looked down the valley to where the ewes and lambs dotted the freshening green meadows. Now there would be no pure-breds, no rosettes.

The sun touched the ridge of the High Moor and sent bars of yellow light through the larch trees, turning the bare branches to russet. It picked the same colour from the mantle feathers of a kestrel as it hovered with quivering wings by the wood's edge. The wings folded and the hawk plunged to flutter momentarily on the ground, before rising with a tiny body clutched between its yellow talons. It flew to the ancient mulberry tree behind the farmhouse to offer the short-tailed vole to his mate, while she vibrated with outstretched wings in an ecstasy of spring courtship. Clegg returned to the house to prepare his solitary meal.

April hazed the larches with a delicate green and brought the elders into full leaf. Celandines starred the woodland floor, and beneath the mulberry tree the snowdrops gave way to tiny wild cyclamen. The earth warmed and the rye grass in the fields by the stream grew an inch in a day and began to ripple and shine as the glossy leaves soaked up the sun. But spring brought no lift to Clegg's spirits and as he drove the tractor into the field to spread the white granules of fertilizer, he felt for the first time since coming to the coombe that he was wasting his life. It was the time to fertilize the hay crop, so he did it, but there was no pleasure in it.

As he walked back to the farmhouse at midday, he could smell the acid scent of growing nettles in every hedge bank, and in the corner of Lower Brownhill the tiny pink flowers of wild orchid pushed up between the grass blades, but the things that once had given him so much joy did so no more. Of all the things on the farm, the orchids had delighted Cathy most; she had looked for them each year in that one corner, for they grew nowhere else.

He stopped for a while and inevitably his thoughts turned to her. There was still no word, but perhaps no news was good news. Maybe she had at last got his letters and was at that moment writing to say they were coming home. She must at least have had his letter, but he decided to send another letter to the last address in Boston with the request that it should be forwarded. He couldn't just sit there and wait for weeks to catch up on him. Why the hell did she have to go off to America at a time like this?

A white car stood in the yard when Clegg pushed through the gate, and a pale young man leant against the bonnet, studying a map. He looked apprehensive as he offered his hand to Clegg.

"I'm from the Water Authority," he said with a diffident smile. "We wrote to you, thought you might like to discuss a few things."

"You'd better come in." Clegg shook hands without enthusiasm and led the way indoors where the young man unrolled the map on the kitchen table.

"You can see the advantages of Ravenscoombe," he began before Clegg could say anything. "Two streams come in - plenty of water, the right rock formation, and this narrow neck here," he pointed to the area marked 'oak coppice'. "That would make an ideal site for a dam."

Clegg watched his performance almost as though it were no concern of his, like an outsider looking at plans for someone else's farm to be drowned. The man from the Water Authority made his case, justified his organisation's decisions and finished with a final, "Now can I answer any questions, Mr Granger?" It was said in a tone that was not inviting.

Clegg stared at the map and shrugged. What could he say? That the land was his? That he had worked, yes, and suffered for it? How much would that count against impermeable rock structures and X gallons of water for Y thousands of people?

"Is there any point in my saying any thing?" he asked.

The young man took out a small notebook. "It's not cut and dried yet, Mr Granger," he said in a less officious tone. "We're expecting to call a public meeting. In the meantime, it's up to you to put up the best case you can. I can assure you that the occupants of the alternative site will do the same."

"Not much of a deal for the farming community, is it?" Clegg murmured. "Either way, some poor devil loses his land and his home."

The young man frowned. "I'm sorry, Mr Granger. No one enjoys this sort of situation." He rolled up the map. "You would receive compensation and a good price for the farm, you know."

"I suppose so," Clegg said absent-mindedly, looking out of the window and wondering how he would be compensated for the grinding work, the heartache and pain he had put into the farm. What price the winter stillness of Colspit or the sight of his flock sunning themselves by the Ravensbourn in the early morning? What value the soar of the buzzards, the silent beat of a barn owl's wing or the harsh bark of a fox in the long December night?

"Suppose so," he repeated.

He watched the white car climb the track to the road and felt no anger, no bitterness, no indignation. He felt nothing, and the fact troubled him.

Clegg wrote his letter but made no mention of the proposed reservoir. When it was done, he called Skipper and walked the length of the coombe to where the enclosed land bordered the High Moor.

Below him, the fields and woods of Ravenscoombe stretched down to the broad water meadows where the river glinted between banks of alder and grey willow. Behind him, the breeze blew from the moor, spiced with the scent of peat. He sat down on the short turf and buried his face in his hands.

The sound of clattering stones made him look down the track to see Tacky's battered trilby emerge from behind the shoulder of the hill. The old man puffed and wheezed as he laboured up the final incline while Tiger raced ahead to push his wet nose into Clegg's face. Tacky set down beside Clegg and took off his hat to mop his brow. Gradually, the wheezing subsided into heavy breathing as the two men looked down over the valley.

Tacky spoke first. "I thought you'd be lookin' out fer the coombe."

"Oh, yes?"

"Ar. 'Tis where us used t' come when things needed sortin'. I saw you making fer th'ead o' the coombe an' knowed you'd come up yer." He looked at Clegg who was still staring towards the little farmhouse and its cluster of grey buildings.

"I mind when I were a boy," Tacky continued, returning his own gaze to the blueing patchwork of distant fields. "I used to sit an' watch fer rabbits with an ol' pin-fire gun as was Grandfather Ackland's. Sometimes when father 'ad given us a 'idin' us come up yer just t' see where the sheep were to, an' sit right in among 'em, like I were one of 'em. An' they ol' yows ud come up an' stand round sniffin' an' I'd say summat to 'em so as they'd know 'twas I, an' us'ld all just lay, wi' they cuddin' an' me watchin' the crows a-sparin' an' a-cawin' over Colspit." He paused. "Ah! You'm thinkin' I be fair mazed sittin' wi' a lot o' sheep, but 'tis a master place fer a bit o' peace."

Clegg pulled a stem of grass and chewed the succulent base. "No, I don't think it's at all foolish." He smiled and twirled the stem between thumb and finger, "and you're right about the peace and quiet."

"Ah! An' I'll tell you summat else. I never could bring meself t' take a pot shot yer, though us seed plenty o' rabbits, an' it weren't only cos it would've scared the sheep. I used to bide till it were near dimmety, then creep along o' that wall and over to the furze brake and get one there. By! An' didn't it set they ol' crows a-rawkin'." The old man chuckled, then fell silent as his thoughts spanned the years.

The shadows that laced the eastern edge of Colspit Wood stretched across adjoining meadows to touch the far hedge banks. Rooks flapped lazily in pairs across orange-tipped clouds, and the moth-shaped whiteness of the barn owl glided up through the gathering river mist.

A little owl called "Kerwik!" and Tacky grunted. "I used to wait fer 'ee," he mused, "an' when the lil' ol' screech owl called, I knew it were passed supper time, an' Mother would scold fer stayin' out so late. But father, 'ee allus used to take my part, why, 'ee used to say, ''ee've only been lookin' out for the coombe, Mother,' an' 'ee used to look across at me and nod."

Clegg picked at the turf with agitated fingers. "I've decided to sell it," he said, studying the fine leaves of sheep's fescue. "Regardless of what happens about the reservoir, I'm going to sell."

CHAPTER 15

AS THE DAYS lengthened, so Tacky's obsession with the grey fox grew. The more he thought about it, the more he became convinced that he had to rid the valley of this omen of bad luck. He began to spend all the daylight hours and a good deal of the night, wet or dry, wandering the fields and woods, looking for footprints and droppings that told him his enemy had passed. He laid snares and tilled gins without success, only stopping short of poison because of the fear that one of the dogs might pick it up. But always the grey shadow eluded him, although he sensed being near many times and had caught glimpses of a swiftly moving shape between the moonlit trunks of Colspit Wood.

Many times, Clegg saw the old man returning to his cottage in the wet dew of morning, his gun under his arm and Tiger at his heels. At other times, only dark imprints on the pearl grey turf showed where Tacky had been astir before sunrise.

In the long May evenings, his bent figure could be seen climbing to the head of the coombe, there to sit among the sheep and gaze out across the valley. At dusk, he would trudge back to the Ashton road and stand as though reluctant to leave the coombe lest it should not be there when he returned in the morning.

In June, the sheep panted in the shade under the weight of their full fleeces. When the yellow "yolk" of grease had risen into the thick curly wool, Clegg and Skipper gathered the flock and brought them into the empty shippon to keep the fleece dry, ready for shearing.

Early next morning, the end of the building was swept clean and a tarpaulin laid on the floor, and with the sheep penned at one end, Clegg started the motor of the shearing machine. Tacky arrived as Clegg caught the first sheep and the two men worked methodically through the flocks, the old man catching the ewes and bringing them to Clegg while the latter sheared, then the shorn animal was pushed out into the yard and Tacky shook out the fleece in one piece on to the tarpaulin and rolled it up, using a twist of wool to tie it. Shearing was a job Clegg normally enjoyed, despite the inevitable aching back, but he allowed himself no feelings of pleasure this time.

The shears clattered and sweat dripped from the end of his nose as he turned the sheep and plied the long sweeping motion of arm and body that made Tacky ask, "Where did you learn to shear like that?"

Clegg straightened his back and released the little Blackface ewe, now strangely goat-like without her thick coat. "I learned it on a special course. It's a New Zealand method," he said, grinning.

The old man shook his head. "I don't reckon they college chaps could learn you much. You'm a fair shearer, though. That last one were off in less than four minutes."

Clegg's spirits lifted for a moment. He had obviously made an impression on Tacky, and the realisation gave him more satisfaction than he would have thought possible.

The shorn flock were driven up to the High Moor where the dreaded sheep fly was less of a menace. Clegg had once found a lost ewe almost eaten alive by the maggots of this pretty iridescent green insect, and the stench and sight of the stricken animal had nearly made him vomit. Thereafter he had been meticulous about dipping the flock twice during the summer months and putting them on to the higher ground whenever possible.

The longest day came and went. The tall rye grass swayed in the hay field as a morning breeze stirred dew-laden cobwebs on fence and hedge and set the broad sycamore leaves fidgeting. By sunup, the gossamer had dried, making the webs once more invisible among the yellow flowers of gorse that crowned the hedge bank. The sun drew up the scents of clover and sweet vernal and warmed the back of the grey fox where he lay curled in the long grass. He stretched full-length and yawned, then dozed again, lulled by the croon of wood pigeons and the lazy hum of insects.

The pigeons stopped abruptly and sat, nervously alert, in the chequered shade of the elms. Far away a tractor droned, and the sound was coming nearer. The pigeons clapped their wings and flew out into the bright sun shine, while the grey fox moved one ear and slept on. Then came a roar and a clatter, and the fox squirmed to his feet, but the tractor and mower were already between him and the wood. He moved further into the crop and settled down to wait.

As the noise moved round the field, small creatures began to move about, scurrying towards the centre and hoped for safety. A rabbit ran within a few inches of the fox, its eyes wide with panic. A hen partridge sat too long with her brood of fledglings and the tractor stopped too late to prevent the slaughter, leaving behind a trail of blood and buff-speckled feathers. Behind the fox, a whirr of bronze wings launched a cock pheasant into the air. There was a shout as the rabbit bolted into the open, a loud crack and another shout. The fox watched the rabbit somersault and he began to run towards the wood.

Clegg saw the fox before it broke cover, and he yelled to Tacky to be ready. The old man moved as quickly as he could to the corner of Colspit

Wood as the grey shape darted for the trees. The gun cracked again, and the fox swerved sideways but kept running. On through the barbed wire and into the brambles, down the side of the quarry, scattering the loose stones and dead leaves, then along the track and into the badger sett, as Tacky poked his head over the fence and looked down.

"I do believe us 'ave got 'un at last?" he said to himself as he ducked between the strands of wire. "Yer, come yer, Tiger!" He called the terrier to heel as he scrambled down the steep slope. At the bottom, he paused to consider the situation. "Now," he said to the dog, "'er's in that ol' sett an' you, my anzum, are goin' to fetch 'un out for us." He bent down to pat the grizzled head. "But us'll 'ave to make certain 'ee stays there till we'm ready for 'un." He took off his jacket and stuffed it into the main entrance to the sett, then he removed his waistcoat, and after taking the watch and chain from the pocket, pushed it into one of the other escape holes. Finally, he stopped the third hole with stones and dead leaves. "There," he said with satisfaction, "'ee'll not get out of there in a 'urry. Now us'll fetch a spade."

The grey fox lay in the scooped-out cavity that had once been the bedding quarters of a badger family. There was still the faint scent of the pied-headed digger clinging to the dead leaves and grass that littered the floor. The fox licked at the bloodstained area of fur just behind his ribs. He nibbled the sore tentatively and felt the small hard lumps beneath the skin which he could not move. Suddenly, the light from the entrance was blocked off, and the fox squeezed up to the nearest bolt hole, but that too was sealed as was the remaining escape route. There was the feared man taint, and the grey fox remembered the events of the short days: the scent of metal and the pain.

He crawled back to the main chamber and lay in the cool dark while his mind worked through the recollections of cause and effect, the nearest he could get to reasoning. He lay waiting and listening. The soil vibrated to the sound of returning footsteps, there was a clink of metal and suddenly the ragged outline of the entrance showed against the greenery outside. The fox turned to watch the patch of light as the strong scent of dog filtered down, then once more the entrance was obscured, but this time by the squat, bow-legged silhouette of the terrier. Snuffling and growling under his breath, Tiger scrambled down the narrow tunnel. He stopped a yard from the fox and barked furiously, his streaming breath filling the confined space. The grey fox lay back his ears and wriggled backwards, the cream fur of his throat pressed to the ground. Step by step, the terrier came on, every now and then making a lunge whenever the grey head lifted. Deeper into the sett they went, where passages crossed and re-crossed and the scent of badger clung to smoothed tree roots. The fox wanted to turn and run down the first opening he came to, but instinct told him he must face an enemy below ground, so he backed away, sensing his opponent's movements in the blackness, feeling for ground that might slope upwards to a possible way out. He paused at the junction of two tunnels and chose the one that turned abruptly towards the surface. He retreated along it until his nose was level with the junction, then stopped. His brush was jammed tight against an outcrop of rock.

Sensing his quarry was cornered, Tiger increased his barking. The fox gulped the foetid air and gave a throaty hiss of defiance. His body coiled against the rock and with a sudden dart forward, he tore at the dog with his long fangs. But the terrier sensed the blow and the fox's teeth missed their mark, catching only the tip of an ear. The dog yelped and pulled backwards, leaving a black remnant between the fox's jaws. Then, hackles bristling, Tiger attacked. Just in time, the fox dropped his head to protect his throat, and the dog's teeth closed on the long snout just above the nose.

Snarling with pain, the fox clawed at the terrier's head, shaking his body from side to side in an effort to free himself. He could taste the blood trickling into his nostrils, a numbness dulled his brain, and still Tiger held on.

The dog braced his short, powerful legs and began to pull, and although much smaller than the fox, he succeeded in dragging the dazed animal to where the tunnel branched. In one last effort, the grey fox tried to turn down the other fork, then suddenly there was a pungent smell of badger and a striped head blocked the way. A gutteral "Yerr!" rumbled out of the old boar badger's throat and at the same time there was the sound of powerful jaws crunching bone. The terrier screamed once, kicked and lay still, then there was silence. The badger sniffed the tainted air loudly, gave a second warning growl and disappeared back down the tunnel. The grey fox ran his long tongue over the torn flesh of his jowl.

Tacky moved a yard and put his ear to the ground once again. He frowned and repeated the movement twice more. There was still no sound. "I don't like it," he said out loud to himself. "They were goin' 'ammer an' tongs a minute ago." He looked around. "Couldn't 'ave found another way out. They'm still in there." Shaking his head, he went to the entrance to the sett. "Yer, Tiger! Yer, boy! Leave 'un." He listened again but there was still no sound, and for the first time, Tacky began to fear for his terrier's safety. Scrambling back, he started to dig above the place where he had last heard Tiger's bark.

Sweat ran down his bare arms and trickled on to the long spade handle, making it slippery to hold. His chest ached with the effort to breathe and small black dots swam in front of his eyes, but he toiled on. Tormented by midges, he worked until his shirt was grey with moisture, stopping only to wipe the spade handle and mop his brow with his red handkerchief. Then the soil fell away and, with a groan, Tacky dropped on his knees as he uncovered the still body of the terrier. He lifted it out on to the fresh soil beside the sett, and for several seconds stared blankly at the bloodstains where the badger's teeth had crushed the spine.

Unbelieving, he turned the dog over, gently stroking the ruffled coat and shaking his head. "Ow'd it 'appen, boy? Tidn' never that fox could've done such a thing, could it?" He looked incredulously towards the sett and blew his nose hard. "That bloody grey fox!" He grabbed the spade and once more attacked the exposed cavity. Something moved under the soil, and he lifted the spade for a final thrust, but the muscles of his chest seemed to tighten and the black dots in front of his eyes ran together into a mist. He swayed for a moment, then sank down beside the body of his terrier.

Clegg finished cutting the field and took the mower back to the farm. He was used to the old man going off on his own and gave no more thought to him until it was time to fetch the cows for the evening milking, a job that Tacky had assumed during the past few weeks. The chore finished, Clegg turned them out again and stood watching the line of pendulous udders sway up the cow path while every now and then a thin thread of saliva would float back where a cow had tossed her head to lick at a fly. Clegg waited until they began to graze, then leant on the gate to see the sun drop below the ridge, watching for the familiar figure to come slowly down the track from the hayfield. But daylight had nearly gone and still Tacky had not returned, so Clegg got out the jeep and drove towards Colspit Wood.

He found them as the last rays burnished the topmost leaves of the oaks. Tacky lay on his back with his eyes closed, a slight wheeze from his chest telling Clegg that he was still alive. The dog was already cold and stiffening. Gently, Clegg lifted the old man into the jeep with the soil-stained jacket round his shoulders. He put the body of the terrier in beside him and drove as carefully as he could towards the farmhouse.

The doctor folded his stethoscope and looked gravely at Clegg. "Heart," he said. "What on earth was a man of his age doing digging out foxes? That's what you said, wasn't it?"

Clegg shrugged. "It's a long story. He just got worked up about the fox taking his poultry," he said lamely.

"Well, I'd rather not move him for a day or two, if that's possible, Mr Granger. In his condition, it might be very tricky. He just needs rest. If I arrange for the nurse to come in regularly, do you think you could cope?"

Clegg shook his head. "I've no one else in the house. I couldn't sit by him all day. I have to look after the farm."

The doctor frowned. "Well, I'll make sure there's someone here during the day if you could see he's comfortable at night. Just until we can't move him into hospital, you see, his heart is just worn out. There's not much medication we can do until he's thoroughly rested, and at this stage the journey to Exeter could be fatal. I'd like to leave him where he is if it is at all possible."

"If you put it like that, I suppose there is no alternative," Clegg replied. "In any case, I suppose I owe the old boy something. It's the least I can do."

"Good. I'll be in first thing in the morning. Let me know immediately if there is any change for the worse." The doctor snapped his bag shut, and Clegg saw him out, then returned upstairs to where Tacky lay in the large double bed. He watched to see that he was breathing steadily, then he made up the bed in the next room.

CHAPTER 16

BLINDED WITH PAIN, the grey fox lay still in the sett as the boar badger retreated to his sleeping quarters. The sound of metal on stone hardly penetrated the fox's numbed senses. Already his left eye was beginning to close and the jagged wound where the terrier's grip had torn his snout caused pain such as he had not experienced before, even in the snare. When the wood was silent, he crawled out and squeezed into the densest part of the bramble thicket to bury his rapidly swelling jowl in the cool leaf mould.

In the cold dawn, he shivered and as the sun rose, the chill turned to fever which wracked his muscles and drew the strength from his body. The air became still and heavy. High in the elms, a lone wood pigeon crooned softly to himself and a myriad of small insects darted in and out of the dappled light, while in the dimness of the thicket, the fox battled with the poisons that had already begun to invade his blood.

Outside the wood, the glare of the noon sun wilted the fresh-cut hay and drew the shimmering heat from the slates of Ravenscoombe Farm. Clegg pulled the curtains in the bedroom where Tacky murmured and grunted in an uneasy sleep. At nine o'clock, the nurse arrived and he was able to bury the remains of the terrier next to the brindled cat before hitching up the hay-turner to the tractor and returning to work.

The rhythmical clank of the machine stirred the fox's dulled brain where he lay in the cleft of Colspit. The sound receded, then came again. As the tractor went round the field, the noises fell into a regular pattern which lulled the stricken animal into deeper sleep where pain and sound became a single throbbing sensation somewhere at the back of his brain.

Shadows deepened, and the leaves of dog's mercury moistened with dew. The clanking stopped, the drone of the tractor faded and for a moment there was silence. Then a little owl called as if giving a signal for the night to begin. The coolness brought the fox back to a half-consciousness and his dry tongue moved tentatively over his torn snout.

He was thirsty. Slowly and painfully, he stood up, then instinctively made his way downhill, feeling the well-trodden animal paths with his pads, for he could see very little and smell nothing. First the soft mould of the thicket, then on to the hard earth under the tall trees. Next, the grassy track that divided the wood in two, then he could feel the carpet of larch needles and at last the damp uneven mud and the sound of running water.

The grey fox stumbled down the bank and into the stream where it ran by the old mill. It carried his limp body under the clapper bridge and tumbled it over boulders before bringing it to rest against the half-submerged trunk of a fallen elm. Once out of the current, the fox gulped air and, with a few feeble strokes, clawed his way along the trunk and pulled himself on to the bank to lie full-length in the black mud.

A woodland hare picked her way among the succulent green shoots to within a few feet of where he lay, but the fox merely watched through one half-closed eye, too weak to move. Other creatures, rabbits, mice and a water vole, fed within easy reach of his jaws as if sensing his inability to move, or perhaps mistaking him for a dead thing. Only the rats showed any interest in the still body, waiting for the cold smell of death before daring to begin the feast.

First light brought a cold mist which hung at ground level, saturating every blade and leaf. The fox shivered but did not move. A wandering ewe snorted and stamped as she caught the faint scent of danger. She was fat and had no lamb at foot, for that had been the grey fox's first meal in Ravenscoombe. She moved on quickly to seek the shade of the wood before the sun rose above the rim of Ashton Down.

The mist lifted to the lowest branches of the alders that lined the bank, then suddenly was gone. Sunlight shafted through the gap in the canopy left by the fallen elm. It warmed the fox and dispelled the chill from his body so that he opened his one good eye, but still he did not move. His torn and blood-clotted nostrils could no longer interpret the scents carried on the air, the one open eye could see no further than the upturned roots of the tree, only the occasional movement of an ear showing that the animal still clung to the slender thread of life.

The bark of a dog made him raise his head. The sound came nearer, and with it the crash of human feet through the underbrush. The fox got unsteadily to his feet and turned to face the noise, backing into the narrow space between the trunk and the ground as Skipper splashed across the stream.

Clegg had been searching for the missing ewe and, with the help of the collie, had traced her to the water's edge. He began to follow the dog across when Skipper gave an excited yelp and darted under the fallen trunk to worry what appeared to be a piece of grey rag. Clegg ran, using the log ash crook to steady himself. As he reached the tree, he saw it was the grey fox and he grabbed Skipper by the scruff to haul him off. He raised the crook, pausing for a moment to aim the blow that would rid the coombe of the ill-omened creature. The fox opened his one eye and in a last gesture of defiance, the mangled lips curled in a snarl. Clegg hesitated. The fox's eye closed in anticipation of the blow, a blow which never came. The ash crook fell harmlessly on to the tree trunk, and Clegg knelt to look at his adversary. The animal was more than half-dead and suddenly Clegg knew he did not want it to die, at least not this way. It came back to him how Tacky had been glad that night in the orchard when he knew it was not the grey fox he had shot, and yet the old man had been so dedicated to hunting the animal. It dawned on Clegg that he too had, at least, become enthusiastic about tracking down the beast, but not to kill a wounded animal in cold blood. He shook his head. There was no logic in his feelings, but then neither was there in those of Tacky Bowden or Josh Huccaby.

After tying up Skipper, Clegg took off his jacket, threw it over the fox and rolled the feebly protesting body in it, eventually tying the bundle with the piece of baling string he always carried in his pocket. This done, he tucked it under his arm, and with an excited Skipper firmly held by the neck, he made his way back to the farm.

He untied the bundle on some fresh straw in one of the more secure loose boxes. The limp grey body stretched full-length and Clegg saw the gunshot wound in the ribs. For a moment, he debated whether to put the animal out of its misery, then he turned, shut the doors and went into the house.

The corner cupboard in the kitchen was the farm medicine chest. Clegg took out a bottle of antiseptic, a syringe and a small dark brown bottle of antibiotic left over from the vet's treatment of an abscess on Skipper's leg. He half-filled the syringe with the antibiotic, then as an afterthought, topped up the rest from another bottle he always kept handy against a whole range of sheep disorders.

"In for a penny, in for a pound," he said to himself as he walked back across the yard. "This'll either kill or cure the poor devil."

He folded the jacket back over the fox's head and held it in place with his knee as he pushed the syringe into the muscle of the hind leg, then he bathed the gunshot wound and removed the lead pellets lodged in the suppurating flesh. Finally, he removed the jacket to look at the animal's lacerated muzzle, but a faint curl of the lip warned him off, and as it looked clean, he decided to leave it alone. He left the coat where it was. It already stank too much of the strong musty colour of fox. He filled a bowl with fresh water and left it near the animal, then making sure the loose box doors were securely bolted, he made his way back to the house.

The nurse smiled as he went in. "He seems to be okay," she said. "He's been asking for you."

Tacky turned his head as Clegg entered. He smiled weakly and the pale dome moved imperceptibly in a gesture of acknowledgement.

"How's it going?" Clegg asked

"Oh, I'm not done fer yet," the old man replied huskily.

There was a long silence during which Tacky closed his eyes and seemed to drift off into sleep. Suddenly, he jerked awake as though remembering. "The grey fox, 'ave you seen 'un ?" Clegg nodded.

Tacky shook his head. "'Er done fer my ol' Tiger. Never knowed nothin' like it before. Never knowed a fox take a terrier below ground. Nothin' like it afore ... dunno what us'll do without th'ol' dog ... " His voice faded.

"I buried him in the garden," Clegg said.

"That's proper. An' you say you've seed th'ol' devil that done it?"

Clegg hesitated for a moment, wondering what the old man's reaction would be. "I've got him in one of the loose boxes at this very minute, and he's a sight nearer dead than alive."

Tacky's eyes opened wider and he pushed himself up on his elbows. "You knock 'un on the 'ead afore 'e gives us any more trouble."

"I can't do that," Clegg said, then grinned. "It's in the middle of Josh's closed season for foxes. He'd never approve."

The old man frowned. "Dear God, don' 'ee start on about Josh 'uccaby. If it 'adn't been fer 'is meddlin' I'd uv 'ad that grey varmint long afore now. Anyway, it's done fer 'im proper." He grunted as he sank back on the pillow. He thought for a while, then said. "I'd like to see 'un."

"Who? Josh?" Clegg asked.

"No, the grey fox. Is 'er real grey?"

Clegg nodded.

"In bad shape?"

Clegg nodded again. "Badly bitten about the face and it's got a shot wound."

The old man gave a satisfied "Ah!", then after a pause, "So ol' Tiger 'ad a real go at 'un then. By! But 'er must be some fox t'kill a good dog like that. Poor ol' Tiger. 'Ee were a rare good dog, proper lil' terrier ... " His voice faded to a whisper.

Clegg stood up. "Well, I'd better get some supper," he said. "I'll let you know how we get on."

Tacky looked up. "You knock 'un on the 'ead," he said in a toneless voice, "You knock 'un on the 'ead."

Before going to bed that night, Clegg looked in the loose box and watched the grey fox by the light of his torch. At first he thought it was dead, then as the beam swung across the straw he saw one eyelid flicker. He switched the torch off and went into the house.

The grey fox lay perfectly still, his body conserving all the energy for the fight that was raging within. Not until first light did he move to ease his cramped muscles. He tried to stand but was too weak and keeled over on to his side and remained stretched out and motionless. At some time, the square of light had appeared again and he sensed the man's presence but did not open his eyes. There were banging noises. The square of light remained after the man had gone away. Sounds came to him, vague and muffled, which he could not interpret and was too ill to fear. For long periods, he slept.

It was night, and he could feel the cool air on his tongue and hear the rustle and movement of things nocturnal. Slowly, he opened his good eye and looked out through the dimmed square at the familiar pattern of a clear sky. He was thirsty, very thirsty and he sensed the nearby bowl of water. It was a metal bowl and metal he feared, yet it contained the thing he craved most. He pushed himself slowly forward until his nose suddenly touched the rim, spilling the cold liquid on to his inflamed snout. He recoiled and lay savouring the moisture with his tongue. It tasted of metal and for a moment fear was stronger than desire, then his tongue found the little pool spilled on the stone floor, and he licked eagerly, spilling more as his snout touched the bowl until the fear subsided, and he lapped the water from inside the vessel. Then he stretched out and slept.

Soon after dawn, the man came again. This time a new thing was put on the floor and although the fox had no sense of smell, he could taste the strong scent of fresh meat with every taste bud on his sensitive tongue. Tentatively, he moved towards it and as he did so, he caught the strong taint of man. He stopped, belly to the ground and head between forepaws, watching the plate with its pile of fresh chopped liver. All day, he lay within a short distance of the meat but did not touch it.

When night came, the man returned and took away the plate, leaving in its place a newly killed young rabbit. The grey fox curled his lip as the man approached, and for several seconds they watched each other in silence, then the man turned with a grunt and went out, closing both doors behind him. As soon as he had gone, the fox crept forward and touched the rabbit with his nose. There was no man taint. He tore open the soft belly and pulled at the warm, sweet entrails. The nourishment brought back the strength to his limbs and he began to pace round the loose box, seeking a way out, but found none. Weakly, he scratched at the space under the door but could make no impression on the stone floor. In his frustration, he threw back his head and screamed into the night.

Clegg woke with a jerk. Someone was moving about next door. He got out of bed to see if Tacky was all right and found the old man standing at the top of the stairs.

"Did you 'ear it?" Tacky asked in a hoarse whisper. "Did you 'ear the fox?"

Clegg took him by the shoulders. "Come on, back to bed. You shouldn't be out. Yes, I heard. It woke me up."

Tacky shook himself free. "Then I weren't dreamin'," he said, taking a step forward. "Come on! Afore 'ee gets away!"

Tacky stretched out a hand for the banister. Clegg grabbed at his shirt, but it swung the old man off balance and before Clegg could get a firmer grip, the stitching gave and Tacky fell headlong down the full flight of stairs.

Clegg straightened Tacky out and put a cushion under his head. The old man looked around at the familiar walls, then he gave a great sigh, closed his eyes and never opened them again.

CHAPTER 17

THEY BURIED TACKY alongside his wife in a churchyard dotted with Bowdens and Acklands going back three hundred years. Gradually, the grief and anger that Clegg felt subsided. Grief for the loss of a friend, anger at the senseless way he died. At the time, he had been tempted to blame the grey fox and had in fact resolved to take the old man's advice and have it put down the next day, but when daylight came, he realised that any fault lay in the man, not the animal, and so he did not call the vet. Often in the following days, it was a topic of conversation between Clegg and Josh who constantly warned him that to free a rogue fox that had also lost its fear of man was asking for trouble. But Clegg could not have it killed, nor could be bring himself to let it go, even though it had begun to gnaw at the bottom of the loose box door, and twice he had found it clawing up the walls halfway to the rafters.

The work on the farm had to continue and Clegg turned the hay again and waited for the contractor to come and bale it while he listened with growing concern to the weather forecast. The night before it was due to be baled, he was awakened by the rumble of thunder over the moor. He lay waiting for the first pit-pat of rain on the window sill, then closed his eyes with a groan and turned over to bury his head in the pillows.

During the next few days, Josh sent Jim over with a spare tractor to help salvage the crop. Eventually, it was baled and carted into the loft, but Clegg knew that it was now poor stuff, and was worried about the moisture content, fearing that it might overheat to the point of catching fire spontaneously. Every day he pushed a metal rod in between the bales and felt the temperature of the end. He sniffed the warm, damp smell and shook his head anxiously.

He decided to ask Josh's advice and arrived at Menaridden to find a worried Isobel standing in the drive.

"I don't know where he is," she replied in answer to his query. "Tom took him up to the farm over an hour ago. He should have been back for lunch by now."

"Well, we'd better go and find out what they're up to," Clegg said, cleaning the passenger seat of the jeep with his handkerchief. Isobel got in and they drove towards the farm.

Clegg pulled up outside the big cattle shed from which came the unmistakable sound of Josh's voice. The shed was empty of cattle and in the centre aisle stood a stocky bay pony held by Jenny the groom. A pair of steps had been placed next to the saddle where Josh was poised precariously with Tom and Jim supporting him under the arms. "Now, lift!" Josh's voice sounded determined, and with a single concerted movement, the two men swung him up and into the saddle.

Isobel gave a little cry of alarm as he steadied himself, and Josh looked up with a frown. "Damn it, Isobel, what are you doing here?" His face relaxed. "Sorry, my dear, it was meant to have been a surprise," then, catching sight of Clegg, "Hello, Clegg, you're just the chap I want to see. Tell you all about it in a minute." He turned to Jenny and, with a nod, said, "Right, move him on." He gritted his teeth as the pony took a step. The girl stopped, but Josh growled, "Go on, damn it." Slowly, step by step, they moved towards the door until they stood in front of the two spectators with Josh grinning from ear to ear. "There you are," he said. "I told you I would ride again."

Isobel made as though to speak but thought better of it. "Oh, I know what you're going to say," he went on, "and I dare say you're right."

Jenny turned the pony and for a moment the grin became a grimace of pain. Isobel sighed as she watched their progress to the far end with Tom and Jim supporting the horseman on either side like a small child on its first ride. The look in Isobel's eyes was a mixture of anguish tinged with pride as she said to Clegg, "You will stay to lunch, won't you?"

Josh was obviously pleased with himself as they sat down to eat. "We've got some good news about the reservoir," he said, helping himself to the cold beef. "Quite a turn-up for the books. Apparently Mrs Wrightson has dug up some information about a rare orchid that grows in the coombe and only a few other places in the whole of Britain."

Clegg nodded. "Yes, that's right. There is a little pink and white orchid that grows in one corner of Lower Brownhill, but I didn't know there was anything special about it. Cathy used ... " He stopped and returned his attention to his plate.

There was a pause while Josh and Isobel exchanged glances, then Josh continued, "Well, it appears that the conservation people are getting quite worked up about it, so that little flower might just do the trick."

Clegg looked thoughtful. "Perhaps what you say is right, but I can't help thinking it's an odd world where a tiny flower carries more weight than the livelihood of men. I'm sure those who farm in the alternative site will think that if the reservoir goes there." He sighed. "Someone loses whichever way it goes."

"Cheer up," Josh grinned. "I was supposed to be bringing good news. Well," he added after a pause, "how are things with you in general?"

"Me?" Clegg looked surprised. "Oh, about the same. I was going to ask you about that hay that's getting a bit hot."

Josh waved his hand impatiently. "No, I meant ... Oh, never mind. Did you know that Briggs knows your father-in-law? Apparently he's an old customer."

Clegg shook his head disinterestedly.

There was a lull in the conversation while Isobel cleared the plates and helped Mabel with the sweet. Josh looked very thoughtful. "Clegg, what are you going to do with yourself? Tacky mentioned that you were thinking of selling up, whatever happened. Is that true?"

Clegg nodded, and Josh glanced at Isobel. "In that case, I ... we, that is, were wondering if you would consider coming into partnership with us here?" He held up his hand before Clegg had a chance to reply. "Now, before you answer, let me explain what I had in mind. I've got to face up to the fact that I won't be a hundred per cent for a very long time, if ever. Briggs will probably take over the hounds if the committee agree - he's been toadying up to me for weeks to put in a good word for him. Tom will hunt hounds on account of Briggs not knowing full cry from riot, and all I have to do is find a good whipper-in. I've got my eye on Bill Petherick's lad. That will be the hunt side of it nicely taken care of, but the farms are not so easy. I need someone I like and trust, someone with a feel for the land and a good eye for stock, and above all someone who's prepared to learn and try new ideas. You fit that to a tee, Clegg. What do you say? Mind I said a partner, not a hired manager. If they don't build the reservoir, we could run the three farms as a single farming company. It's got great possibilities, Clegg, and we could do Ravenscoombe up and - "

"And what if they do build the reservoir?" Clegg interjected.

"Well, then we could look into the possibility of your taking Higher Ford. I've asked John and Polly Brimblecombe to move into the cottage here. Running that farm has really got too much for them."

Clegg looked thoughtful, "You seem to have got everything nicely worked out, and I must say, it sounds very attractive," he said slowly, "but I'm afraid there's one snag."

Isobel reached out and put a hand on his arm. "We know, Clegg," she said, "and we hope that things will straighten themselves out soon. But I hope it won't take too long. You see, there's a little place in Italy that Josh and I plan to get reacquainted with and we'd feel happier if Menaridden was left in the hands of a co-director." She smiled as Josh took the hand she removed from Clegg and squeezed it.

"Oh, incidentally, if you're wondering who first put the idea into my head," Josh said, "it was dear old Tacky. Who would have thought he had such hidden depths?"

Clegg smiled. "Who indeed," he said.

On the way home, Clegg's mind buzzed with the plans, the hopes and the forebodings that the offer raised. He felt more than ever that his life had reached a crossroads, that the only road he could take would be the one with Cathy, and if that road did not lie in Ravenscoombe, well ...

He pulled up in the yard but avoided going straight into the house. Instead, he let Skipper out and set off for the head of the coombe, for he needed somewhere to think.

They walked through Lower Brownhill and sure enough the little pink and white flowers were there. Clegg turned his attention to the rest of the field and noted with satisfaction that the bracken was shorter and less dense than in previous years. The regular cutting was obviously taking effect. He considered the possibility of using the new chemical spray next year, then decided against it. Those orchids had suddenly become very precious. It also occurred to him that there might not be a next year.

He looked down towards Cotspit and wondered what would become of its inhabitants if they flooded the coombe: the badgers, voles, foxes, rabbits. Would they sense the danger and get out before the water came, or would they wait to be cut off and be drowned with the oaks? Would the brown trout soon glide among the branches of the elms where now the buzzard sat, or would that little flower save them all? It disturbed him that Man, playing God, had it in his power to create a natural catastrophe and would do so because of the overabundance of his own species and the belief that the cheapest way must necessarily be the best.

They reached the top of the coombe. Cragg Tor stood black against an orange-tinged sky which held, for a moment, the raven's silhouette as it glided to roost under the topmost boulder. It was the time when greens turn to grey, and grey to black; when field outlines blur with long shadows and river mists creep over reeded meadows. "Dimpsey" or "Dimmity" Tacky had called it. At Dimpsey, sound carries a long way. A dog barked in the next valley but had no heart in it and tailed off into silence. The sound of a woman's voice drifted across the coombe, stirring memories which Clegg blotted out with a curt. "Some damned woman lost her dog, I expect."

From the direction of Trenden Wood came the harsh bark of a fox, and Clegg thought of the grey fox padding round his man-made prison.

Perhaps Tacky had been right, perhaps it was an omen of bad luck. In the between light of Dimpsey, he could almost believe it himself, and yet wasn't it the fox that had drawn Tacky, Josh and himself together, like a grey thread woven into the pattern of their lives?

Certainly, that pattern had been dramatically altered. He thought of Tacky and the old man's obsession with hunting the fox, or was that just an excuse to once again walk the fields and woods of Ravenscoombe? And what of the outcome? Well, it was no bad thing, Clegg reflected, for an old man to die in the house he was born in. And there was Josh. He too had changed, not just physically but in his attitude to other people, particularly Isobel. But had it affected himself, Clegg Granger, who had thought he could stand alone? Who was he to say? If only he could talk to Cathy ...

A little owl's grating "kerwick" broke his reverie. "Time to go," he said to Skipper, and in the gathering darkness they set off down the narrow track.

As they came in sight of the farm, Clegg suddenly stopped, for through the trees he could see a point of light. He knew no lamps had been left alight, and apprehension made him break into a run. "Oh, God, not fire, not the hay!" he groaned, quickening the pace until the farmhouse was in full view. Then he stopped again, at once both relieved and perplexed. There was no fire. The light came from the kitchen window with the steady brilliance of the pressure lamp, and there was somebody moving about inside. Then the door opened and a figure stood silhouetted for a moment. Clegg began to run and a tightness gripped his throat, stifling the yell to a croak. He splashed through the stream without bothering to find stepping stones, clawing over the hedge to cross the garden where at last the one word exploded into a hoarse bellow.

"Cathy!"

She met him in the doorway, and for a moment he was afraid to move lest the vision should disappear, then she was in his arms, real and warm.

"Oh, Clegg, I've been calling for you for over an hour. Where were you? Look at you! You're bleeding and absolutely soaked!" She stood back at arm's length while Clegg noticed for the first time that his hand was torn by brambles and his trousers, saturated to the knees, had left a small pool on the flags. "Come on," she said gently. "Let's get you sorted out before we have some supper, then we can talk."

Clegg followed her to the sink. It was just like her, he thought, so matter of fact you'd have thought she had been away for a week's holiday. "Cathy ... " he began, but she turned and put a hand over his lips.

"No, let me speak first," she said quietly. "I've come home, Clegg. I know about the reservoir, and I know about the possibility of a partnership or something, but that's not why I've come. I've discovered that ... well ... I just can't do without you. It's as simple as that." She smiled and put her arms round his neck. "I guess I love you, and if that means Ravenscoombe or anything else, then I'm prepared to give it a try."

He lifted her head and kissed her. "You know," he said softly, "I'd come to the same conclusion about you." He paused and looked around. "But where's Stephen?"

Cathy pointed to the ceiling. "He was tired out," she whispered.

Clegg, nodded, then looked up suddenly. "And how on earth did you know about the reservoir and the partnership offer? I've never mentioned it."

Cathy tilted her head and grinned. "Oh, your Huckersly - "

"Huccaby," Clegg corrected.

"Yes, that's it. Huccaby. Well, he is a very determined man and not a little devious. Apparently, he knows one of Daddy's customers, so he got an introduction and persuaded Daddy to send on your letters and arrange for us to come home. All I can say is, he must have spun quite a yarn. But you can tell him that it was all a waste of time," she added tartly. "You see, I had already decided."

She stopped speaking and listened. There was a thump from above, then the clump of bare feet on the stairs and a small pyjama-clad figure hurtled across the room.

"Dad! Dad! You weren't here! We've had a t'rific holiday! I haven't had to go to school ... "

"Steady on, steady on, one thing at a time!" Clegg sat down and swung the boy on to his knee, but Stephen chattered on: "We went on a plane, Dad ... Did you catch the fox? ... Dad, you're all wet."

Clegg laughed. "That's what comes of running through streams without looking where you're going," he said, ruffling the boy's hair. "And I have got the latest instalment of the saga of the grey fox. That well-known lamb and chicken thief is at this very moment under safe lock and key in a loose box outside."

Stephen wriggled to his feet. "Cor! Can I go and see him now? Can I, Mum?" He looked at Cathy.

"Only if you put your trousers and a woolly on, then we'll all go," she said. "I want to see this animal that has obsessed your father."

"What does 'obsessed' mean, Dad?"

"Just that he seems to have taken up a lot of my time."

The boy left the room as rapidly as he had entered, and Cathy began to put on her coat. "What are you going to do with it, Clegg?" she asked.

Clegg shrugged. "I've put off that decision for over a week. I suppose the sensible thing would be to get the vet to put him down."

"Oh no!" Cathy exclaimed. "Not after catching it alive. That would be like an execution. You couldn't do that."

Clegg stood up. "Tell you what," he said, "you and Stephen can decide."

"Decide what, Dad?" Stephen stood in the doorway.

"What to do with the fox."

"Can't I keep it as a pet? I'd look after it."

Clegg shook his head. "I'm afraid it's probably too old to tame as a pet, Stephen. We could perhaps keep it in some sort of a pen."

"You mean like in a zoo?" The boy frowned.

"Yes, something like that. A wildlife park or the like. Anyway, come and see him."

Together, they walked across the yard to the loose box and Clegg shone the torch through the wire netting. The fox lay on Clegg's old jacket in the corner. As the beam crossed the floor, he raised his head, the dark-tipped ears flattened, and a scarred lip curled very slightly to show the points of canine teeth.

"He's been hurt," Cathy whispered.

Clegg nodded. "He was half-dead when I found him."

"Can we go in, Dad?"

"Yes, if you keep quiet. He scares pretty easily."

Cathy hesitated. "Clegg, I wonder if we should. Will he bite, I …?" She looked at Clegg questioningly.

He smiled. "Don't worry. He's much more scared of you than you are of him. He's not likely to do anything as long as you don't try to touch him." Clegg looked down at Stephen to make sure the boy understood, then he unbolted the door and they went inside.

Cathy was the first to speak. "He's nearly the colour of Aunt Dorothy's fur stole. Haven't I heard that grey foxes are supposed to bring bad luck?"

"I knew somebody who thought so," Clegg said slowly, "and for him, it was true." He turned to Stephen. "Well, now you've seen him, what do you think we ought to do with him?"

The boy watched the fox in silence, then slowly and deliberately he turned and pushed open the door. Clegg nodded and with a half-smile, he took Cathy's hand and led her outside. The three of them stood in the dark, and for several seconds, nothing moved, then there was the faintest rustle inside the loose box and a shadow glided silently across the yard and under the field gate. Clegg switched on the torch. A pair of slant amber eyes blinked once … twice, and then disappeared.

"Where will he go, Dad?" Stephen's voice was a hoarse whisper.

Clegg grinned. "Who can tell, son? Grey foxes are supposed to just vanish."

"Do you think he'll ever come back, Dad?"

Clegg put an arm round Cathy's waist and drew her close to him. "No, Stephen, I don't think we shall ever see a grey fox in our valley again."

Arm in arm, they walked back to the farmhouse. Lights downstairs wavered and moved upstairs. The barn owl drifted through the orchard to perch like a sentinel on the loft roof until the lights went out and he could glide down to hunt the rat runs among the farm buildings. The screech owl called, and Ravenscoombe gave itself to the night.

Beyond the coombe's rim, the moon drew on its blanket of mist, curling it round the tall stones of Hods Barrow. At the summit of the tumulus, a grey shadow moved into the circle of granite, and for a moment the mist parted and the shadow took form. The fox stood, one forefoot raised, looking back from whence he had come, then, as the mist closed in on him once more, he turned and was gone.

www.ingramcontent.com/pod-product-compliance
Lightning Source LLC
Chambersburg PA
CBHW060805210726
48292CB00013B/1768